C2000004597715

NRO8

1 7

THE
TWELVE NIGHTS
OF CHRISTMAS

BY
SARAH MORGAN

First published in Great Britain 2010
Harlequin Mills & Boon Limited,
Eton House, 18-24 Paradise Road, Richmond, Surrey TW9 1SR

© Sarah Morgan 2010

ISBN: 978 0 263 21531 1

Harlequin Mills & Boon policy is to use papers that are natural,
renewable and recyclable products and made from wood grown in
sustainable forests. The logging and manufacturing process conform
to the legal environmental regulations of the country of origin.

Printed and bound in Great Britain
by CPI Antony Rowe, Chippenham, Wiltshire

THE
TWELVE NIGHTS
OF CHRISTMAS

To Kimberley Young:
seven years and forty-two books together.
Thank you. xx

CHAPTER ONE

'I NEVER thought this moment would come, Pietro. Let's celebrate.' Rio Zaccarelli sat back as the vintage champagne was poured into his glass. Across the table, his lawyer opened his case and handed him a sheaf of papers.

'I'm not celebrating until this one is in the bag. How did you get a table here? I've never seen so many rich, powerful people in one place.' Pietro glanced discreetly over his shoulder, his gaze skimming the other diners. His eyes widened as he focused on a man in a dark grey suit. 'Isn't that—?'

'Yes. Don't stare or you'll have security teams swarming over your lunch.' Rio flicked through the papers, scanning the contents. As he reached for his champagne he noticed that his hand shook slightly and he wrenched back his emotions, forcing himself to treat this like any other business deal. 'You haven't eaten here before?'

'I've been waiting a year to get a table at this restaurant and you do it in one phone call. There are times when I wish I had your influence.'

'Complete this deal and I'll get you a table. That's a promise.' *Complete this deal and I'll buy you the restaurant.*

'I'll hold you to that. You have to sign on the back page.' Pietro handed him a pen and Rio signed the documents with a bold scrawl.

'As usual, I owe you—for your discretion as well as your

astonishing legal brain. Order the lobster. It's sublime and you've more than earned it.'

'Thank me when it's all signed and sealed and not before. I've learned not to celebrate until the ball is in the net. It's been a hard fight and this may still not be finished.' The lawyer took the wedge of papers and slipped them into his briefcase. 'The stakes are high. They haven't stopped fighting, Rio. They don't want you to win this.'

'I'm aware of that.' A red mist of anger coloured his vision and his fingers tightened on the delicate stem of the champagne flute. The tension was like steel bands around his body. 'I want to be kept updated, Pietro. Any changes, phone my personal line.'

'Understood.' Pietro snapped his case shut. 'This deal could still blow itself apart. The most important thing is that you need to keep yourself whiter than fresh snow between now and Christmas. Don't get yourself so much as a parking ticket. Not a blemish. Not a rumour. My advice as a friend who knows you? Find an isolated ski lodge and lock yourself away. No liaisons with women, no kiss and tell stories—for the time being, sex is off the agenda.'

Rio, who hadn't gone ten days without sex since he'd lost his virginity, kept his face expressionless. 'I'll be discreet.'

'No.' Pietro leaned forward, switching from friend back to lawyer in the blink of an eye. 'If you want this deal watertight, then discretion isn't enough. I'm saying no sex, Rio. Unless it's married sex. If you happen to suddenly fall for a decent, wholesome girl whose entire objective in life is to love you and give you babies, that might actually help your case—' he gave a faint smile and spread his hands in a fatalistic gesture '—but, knowing you as I do, there's not much chance of that.'

'None at all. There's no such thing as a decent, wholesome girl and if there were she'd undergo a personality change the moment she met me,' Rio drawled. 'Within minutes she'd be thinking about prenuptial agreements and record breaking divorce settlements.'

Pietro picked up the menu. 'I don't blame you for being cynical, but—'

'I understand you. No sex. Sounds like I'm in for an exciting Christmas.' Rio thought of the Russian ballerina who was currently waiting in his apartment, lying on silk sheets, waiting for the visit he couldn't risk making.

He'd send her diamonds and give her the use of his private jet to fly home to Moscow for Christmas. They could pick up their relationship in the New Year. Or not. Realising that he wasn't bothered either way, he frowned.

Perhaps it was a good job he had an urgent business trip to make. He could work off his excess energy in other ways.

His eyes blank of expression, Rio stared out of the glass sided restaurant that had views over the centre of Rome, watching the crazy traffic fighting for space on the streets below.

There was nothing he wouldn't do to achieve the outcome he wanted. Even denying his libido for a short time.

Pietro put down the menu and picked up his glass, a hint of a smile on his face. 'I have a feeling this will be the hardest thing you've ever done. Go somewhere there are no women. I hear Antarctica is sparsely populated at this time of year.'

'I have to fly to London on business.'

'You are confronting Carlos?'

'I'm firing him,' Rio said coldly. 'His appointment was a mistake. I've had a full report from the external management consultant I put into the hotel. I need to deal with the situation before his appalling mismanagement affects the reputation of my company.'

'I don't suppose I can persuade you to wait until after the deal is signed?'

'Carlos cannot affect this deal.'

'In theory I would agree, but—' frowning, his lawyer put his glass down slowly '—this has been a difficult fight and we're not there yet. I'm uneasy.'

'That's why I'm paying you such an astronomical sum. I pay you to be uneasy, so that I can sleep.'

Pietro lifted an eyebrow. 'Since when did you start sleeping? You work harder than I do. Especially at this time of year. I assume you're planning to work right through Christmas?'

'Of course.'

The lawyer picked up the warm, crusty bread roll from his side plate and broke it in half. 'Why do you hate this time of year so much?'

A cold, sick feeling rose in his stomach. Aware that, as always, he was the focus of attention in the restaurant, Rio sat still, his features carefully composed. Catching the eye of a pretty European princess who had been gazing at him across the restaurant since he'd arrived, he gave a brief nod of acknowledgement. Desperate for distraction, he contemplated accepting her blatant invitation, but then he remembered Pietro's warning. No sex. Whiter than white.

Instead, he drained his champagne glass and formulated an answer to the question. 'Why do I hate Christmas? Because everyone uses Christmas as an excuse to stop work,' he lied smoothly, wrestling down his emotions with sheer brute force. 'And I'm a demanding boss. I hate time wasters, you know that. But I appreciate all the hours you've put into this deal and I will heed the advice. Until this deal is closed, the only person sleeping in my bed will be me.'

'It might make for a boring Christmas, but that is exactly the way it should be. I'm serious, Rio. Stay indoors. The only things you should be touching are your laptop and your phone.' Pietro looked him in the eye. 'Don't underestimate how much could still go wrong.'

'Whiter than white,' Rio purred, a faint smile touching his

mouth. 'I can do that if I really concentrate. Anyway, I'm not likely to meet a woman who interests me in London. Shall we order?'

'You can't do this to me! You can't just throw me out of my home! I can't *believe* you changed the locks when I was out. Don't you have any human feeling?' Evie grabbed the man's arm, almost slipping on the snow and ice as he shrugged her off and dropped his tools back into his bag.

'Life's tough. Blame your landlord, not me. Sorry, love.' But he didn't look sorry and Evie felt the panic rise as the enormity of the situation hit her.

'It's only twelve days until Christmas. I'll never find anything else at this short notice.'

The emotions she'd been suppressing for six stressful weeks suddenly broke through the front she'd been presenting to the world.

This was supposed to have been her wedding day. Tonight she would have been flying to a romantic hotel in the Caribbean on her honeymoon to make a baby. Instead, she was on her own in a big, cold city where no one seemed to care about anyone else. It was snowing and she was homeless.

'At least let me get my things.' Not that she had much. The few things she'd brought with her could probably fit into one rubbish bag.

Even as the thought wafted through her mind, the man gestured to a black bin liner leaning against the door.

'Those are your things.' The man snapped his bag shut. 'Good job you haven't got much stuff.'

Evie wondered what was good about not having much stuff. She'd thought moving to London would be exciting and full of opportunities. She hadn't realised how expensive it would be. Everything cost a fortune. And she hadn't realised how lonely it would be living in a city. She couldn't afford a social life. When a few of the girls at work had invited her out, she'd had to refuse.

The snow fluttered onto her head and neck and Evie huddled deeper inside her coat, her spirits as low as the temperature.

'Just let me stay here tonight, OK? I'll try and find some-where tomorrow—' She felt as though she was holding every-thing together by a single fragile thread. It had been that way since the day Jeff had texted her to tell her the wedding was off. Concerned about her grandfather's distress, she'd taken refuge in the practical, returning presents with polite notes at-tached, cancelling the church and the venue, explaining to all the well-wishers who arrived at the house. She'd told herself that she'd shed her tears in private, but she'd discovered that cancelling a wedding was almost as much work as organising one, without any of the excitement to drive you forward. By the time she'd fallen into her bed at night she hadn't had the energy to cry. 'Please—it's going to be impossible to find somewhere else to live this close to Christmas.'

'It's a dog eat dog world, love.'

Evie recoiled. 'I love dogs. I'd *never* eat a dog! And it's supposed to be the season of goodwill.'

'I feel plenty of goodwill. Thanks to landlords like yours, I have a job.'

'Well, it's nice to know I'm supporting someone through the credit crunch—' Feeling a vibrating in her pocket, Evie dug out her phone, her anxiety doubling when she saw the number. 'Just wait there a moment and don't go anywhere because I have to answer this or he'll worry—he's very old and—Grandpa? Why are you calling in the middle of the day? Are you OK?' She prayed he hadn't had another one of his turns. It was one thing after another. Her life was unrav-elling faster than a pulled thread in a sweater. She'd wanted so badly to make him proud. Instead, all she was going to do was worry him.

'Just checking up on you because I saw the pictures of the snow on the news.' Her grandfather sounded frail and Evie tightened her grip on the phone, hating the fact that he was getting older.

He was the person she loved most in the world. She owed him everything. 'I'm fine, Grandpa.' She shivered as more flakes of snow found their way inside her coat. 'You know I love the snow.'

'You always did. Built any snowmen yet? You always loved building snowmen.'

Evie swallowed. 'I…I haven't had the chance yet, Grandpa. Soon, I hope. There's a huge park opposite the hotel where I'm working. It's crying out for a snowman.' She didn't tell him that no one paused to build a snowman in London. Everyone was too busy rushing from one place to another.

'Are you at work now? I don't want to bother you if you're at work, dealing with some high-powered celebrity.'

High-powered celebrity?

'Well…er…' Her face scarlet, Evie moved away from the man who had just tipped her life into a rubbish bag and wondered whether the lie she'd told about her job was about to come back to bite her. It was one thing trying to protect her grandfather, but she'd probably gone a little over the top. Or possibly more than a little. 'Grandpa—'

'I boast to everyone about you. I'm so proud of you, Evie. I told that stuffy Mrs Fitzwilliam in the room next door to mine, "My granddaughter has got herself a brilliant high-powered job. She may have been left standing at the altar—"'

Evie pressed her fingers to her aching forehead. 'It wasn't at the altar, Grandpa. No one got as far as the altar—'

'"—but she picked herself up and now she's a receptionist at the smartest hotel in London and she never would have had that opportunity if she'd married useless Jeff." He was nothing but a dreamer. And he wasn't good enough for you,

you know that, don't you? He was wet, and you don't want a man who is wet. You need a *real* man.'

'Any man would be a start,' Evie muttered under her breath, 'but fat chance of that.'

'What was that?'

'Nothing.' For once grateful for her grandfather's hearing aid, she changed the subject quickly. 'Are you OK? Are they treating you all right there?' Although he'd persuaded her he wanted to go into the same home as his closest friend, she still wasn't comfortable with the idea.

'My bones are aching in the damp weather and they make too much fuss here.'

Evie smiled. 'It will be summer soon. And I'm glad they're fussing.'

'I wish I could see you at Christmas but I know it's too far for you to come for just one day. I'm worrying about you on your own. I miss you, Evie.'

Flattened by homesickness, Evie felt a lump settle in her throat. 'I miss you, too. And I'll try and come up as soon as I can. And don't worry. I'm fine.' She pushed the words past her cold lips and then waved her hand frantically as the man loaded his tools into his van. Was he really just going to drive away and leave her here, standing on a snowy pavement in the dark? What had happened to chivalry? Her fiancé broke up with her by text and this man was about to leave a vulnerable woman alone in a big, scary city with nowhere to spend the night. Where were all the knights in shining armour when you needed them? Her grandfather was right—she needed a real man. Down with rats, wimps and cowards.

'So how's the job going?' Her grandfather used his most bracing voice. 'I told Mrs Fitzwilliam that you have Hollywood stars staying and that you'll be meeting and greeting them personally. That shut her up. Nosy old madam.'

Evie didn't know whether to laugh or cry. She was going to be struck down for lying to her grandfather. On the other hand, the alternative option was disappointing and worrying him. And she *did* 'meet and greet' guests. Sort of. If she met someone, she greeted them, didn't she? The fact that they usually ignored her didn't count. 'The job's great, Grandpa. Brilliant.' She'd been demoted and the slimy hotel manager had made a pass at her but, apart from that, it was all perfect.

The man started the engine and Evie sprinted across the pavement to stop him, her feet slithering on the ice. 'Wait—'

Her grandfather was still chatting. 'I've been watching the shares of Zaccarelli Leisure. They're soaring. You picked a winner there, Evie. At least your job is safe.'

No. No, it wasn't safe. Her entire existence was balancing on a knife edge.

Evie had a sudden urge to confess that the manager had tried it on with her, but stopped herself in time. She didn't want to upset her grandfather. And she also had a sneaking worry that he might somehow get on a train, find his way to London and deal with Carlos Bellini personally. Despite his eighty-six years, her grandfather was a real man.

'My job is…it's…well, it's great,' she said firmly. 'Really good.'

'Going to any Christmas parties? I'm sure you'll be able to have your pick of men if you do! And you won't be able to make it through the Christmas season without singing *The Twelve Days of Christmas* at the top of your voice. You know you always love doing that.'

'No parties planned. And I'm not quite ready to meet another man yet, Grandpa.' Dragging the bag behind her, Evie slithered towards the van. As she let go of it, the top gaped open and her tiny silver Christmas tree tumbled into the snow and slush. 'Don't worry about me. I'm fine.' A lump in her throat, she stared at her Christmas tree, which was now lying in a puddle. Her whole life felt as though it was sinking into a puddle.

'Don't hang around, Evie. I'm not getting any younger. Next year I want to be bouncing a great-grandchild on my knee.'

What? 'I'll do my best, Grandpa.' Wondering how on earth she was going to fulfil that particular wish when she couldn't find a man who wanted to talk to her, let alone sleep with her, Evie forced out a cheery goodbye and dropped the phone back in her pocket.

As she retrieved the dripping Christmas tree, the man drove off, showering her with slush.

It was snowing steadily and Evie was just wondering whether it was worth wading through the contents of the bag to find her umbrella when her phone rang again.

'Why am I suddenly the most popular person in the world?' Looking at the number flashing on her phone, she groaned. *Oh, no.* 'Tina? I know I'm late, but I've—' she flinched as her boss gave her a sharp lecture '—yes, I know Salvatorio Zaccarelli is arriving tomorrow and—yes, I know it's important because he's looking at the way the hotel is run and we're all under scrutiny. Yes, I know I was lucky you gave me another chance with this job when you could have fired me—' She gritted her teeth as she listened. 'I—yes, the Penthouse will be perfect, I promise—I'm lucky that Carlos wants me to do the job personally—I do know Mr Zaccarelli is the most important guest we ever have—I know he doesn't suffer fools and won't tolerate anything less than perfection—' *the guy was obviously a cold, heartless pig* '—I feel the same way,' Evie lied, making a mental note not to be anywhere near the scary, ruthless tycoon when he arrived at the hotel. The way she was feeling at the moment, she'd probably punch him. That was one 'meet and greet' that was *not* going to happen. If she saw him coming she was going to dive for cover.

Tina was still talking and Evie slithered her way towards the bus stop, the rubbish bag banging against her legs, her clothes soaked through. Snow landed on her hair and water dripped down her neck. '—Festive? Sparkling? Yes, I'm going to decorate the Christmas tree—I'll be there ever so soon, but I just need to—' she broke off; *I just need to find somewhere to sleep tonight when I come off my shift at midnight* '—catch a bus. The buses are mad because of Christmas, but I'm on my way now.' All she ever did was tell lies, Evie thought, struggling with the bag. She lied to protect her grandfather from more worry and she lied to Tyrannosaurus Tina because, until she'd found something better, she couldn't tell the woman where to stick her job. Maybe she should suggest to scary Salvatorio Zaccarelli that the first person he should fire was the manager of his flagship hotel.

As she sat on the crowded bus, jammed between stressed out Christmas shoppers, Evie wondered if she should have just told her grandfather the truth. That London was lonely. That she missed him. That she'd been demoted after just days in her new job by a boss who hated her. Apparently, she'd been too friendly.

Evie sighed, well aware that she'd probably been a little too desperate for human company. But she still didn't understand why that was a crime. As a receptionist in a hotel, how could you be too friendly? Anyway, she had no opportunity to be friendly now because, as a member of the housekeeping staff, she didn't often meet any guests. She didn't meet anyone. She'd taken to talking to herself as she cleaned bathroom mirrors.

Trying to take her mind off it, Evie picked up a discarded magazine and flicked through the pages, staring gloomily at the slender models wearing the magazine's recommendations for glittery dresses perfect for the party season. Apparently, silver was bang on trend. Absently, she picked the one she would have worn if she had money and had actually been invited to a party. Shimmering silver, she thought, with diamonds and swept up hair. Except that she'd look ridiculous dressed like that.

Face it, Evie, you're a bit of a freak.

Hearing Jeff's voice in her head, she dropped the magazine back on the seat, jumped off the bus and walked towards the back entrance of the prestigious hotel that provided a bolthole for the world's rich and famous. She was just wondering where she was going to hide a rubbish bag when a sleek black Mercedes drove through a puddle and muddy water sprayed over her tights and shoes.

'Oh, for—' Hopping to one side, soaking wet, Evie glared after the expensive car, imagining the warm, luxurious interior. 'Thanks a lot. Just as long as you're comfortable in your cosy, rich cocoon.' Her eyes widened in disbelief as she read the number plate. 'TYC00N.' Drenched and shivering, she wondered what it was like to live a life of luxury, filled with diamonds, shimmering silver dresses and ostentatious car accessories.

'Hi, Evie, you're late.' A colleague hurried past her in a cloud of perfume and hairspray. 'You've already missed the staff briefing. Tina said you were to go straight to the Penthouse because she doesn't have time to waste with you. The big boss is arriving tomorrow. Rumour has it that he is going to axe anyone who doesn't fit. Even Creepy Carlos is nervous. Personally, I can't wait to see Rio Zaccarelli in person. He's the most stunningly good-looking man I've ever seen.'

Chilled to the bone, Evie sneezed. 'You've never seen him.'

'I've seen him in pictures. Red-hot Rio, that's what we're calling him.'

'Ruthless Rio is what *I'm* calling him,' Evie muttered and her colleague frowned at the bag in her hand.

'Since when have you been responsible for dealing with the trash?'

'Oh, I like to be helpful. Versatile, that's me—' Evie pinned a rigid grin on her face, refusing to admit that she was carrying her home around. Like a snail, she thought, as she followed the girl through the glass door and into the plush, privileged warmth of a different life. Maybe there was a number plate that spelled out DISASTER. She could stick it on her back to warn people she was coming.

Hiding her bag in the basement behind some large pipes, Evie took refuge in the peaceful elegance of the Penthouse suite. She felt so utterly miserable that, for the first time since her aborted wedding and humiliating demotion, she was relieved that she wasn't on Reception, having to smile and be cheerful. She didn't want to meet and greet. She just wanted to curl up in a ball and not emerge until her life had improved.

The warm, spacious luxury of the top floor suite made her feel instantly calmer and Evie looked around her wistfully. Two deep white sofas faced each other across a priceless rug and flames flickered in the fireplace. Huge floor to ceiling windows gave views over Hyde Park and the elegant buildings of Knightsbridge.

Someone had put a large fir tree next to the grand piano and boxes of decorations were neatly stacked, ready for Evie to create a perfect Christmas.

A perfect Christmas for someone else.

'Imagine spending Christmas somewhere like this,' she murmured, talking to herself as she explored the Penthouse suite. 'Talk about how the other half live.'

Feeling incredibly down, Evie set to work decorating the tree, trying not to think about the times she'd done the same thing with her grandfather. Last year they'd shared a wonderful Christmas. She'd baked Christmas cake and Christmas puddings and roasted a turkey just for the two of them. They'd eaten leftovers for weeks. Turkey curry, turkey soup, turkey sandwiches—

Only a few weeks later, her grandfather had suffered a mini stroke and she'd had no choice but to agree to let him go into the home where his friends were. They'd sold his cottage to pay the exorbitant fees and now she was miles away in a city where no one spoke to anyone except to ask directions.

And she had nowhere to sleep tonight. The thought terrified her and for a moment she considered confessing to Tina and asking if she had any free rooms. Imagining the response she'd get, a hysterical laugh bubbled up from the cauldron of panic that was simmering inside her. Tina would simply remind her that one night in the cheapest room in this hotel was more than her monthly salary.

Merry Christmas, Evie.

She worked without a break, twisting lights through the branches of the enormous tree, hanging glittering silver baubles and filling vases with elaborate displays of holly. Then she started to clean the Penthouse. She was only halfway through when the door opened and Carlos, the hotel manager, strode in.

Evie was immediately on the defensive, horribly aware that she was alone with him and that her mobile phone was in her coat pocket at the other end of the room.

She'd avoided him since the day he'd tried to kiss her and she stood warily, her mind scrambling through her options. They were pitifully few. He ran the hotel and held her future in the palm of his hand. Unfortunately, he'd made it clear that he wanted to hold other bits of her in the palm of his hand, too.

His hair shone greasily under the lights and Evie shuddered, bracing herself for criticism.

Was he looking for an excuse to fire her?

'It looks perfect. Incredibly Christmassy. Just what I wanted for Rio.' Something about his smile made her uneasy.

'You're sure you like it?'

'Absolutely.' His eyes trailed over her body. 'You're wet.'

Evie stood rigid, wondering why the only man to pay her any attention had to be a total creep.

'It's snowing. I had to wait for a bus.'

'I don't want my staff catching pneumonia. Take a hot shower.'

She felt herself blush. 'I can't afford the time. I still have loads to do and my shift ends in thirty minutes.'

'You're on again first thing tomorrow morning.' Carlos frowned. 'Stay here tonight. That way, you can start work straight away. I want everything perfect.'

He was giving her permission to stay in the hotel?

Unable to believe her luck, Evie almost sobbed with relief. 'That would be helpful,' she said casually. 'Do we have a spare room?'

'No, we're full. But you can stay here. In the Penthouse.'

Evie looked at him stupidly. *'Here?'*

'Why not? Rio isn't arriving until tomorrow afternoon. Your shift ends at midnight and begins again at seven in the morning. It makes perfect sense for you to stay here. Sleep on top of the bed if it bothers you. I'll make sure you're not disturbed.'

Evie stared at him, her instincts on full alert. 'You're suggesting that I stay in the *Penthouse*?'

'Why not? It isn't doing anyone any harm and I owe you a favour.' He hesitated. 'Evie, I apologise if I came on a little strong a few weeks ago. I misread the signals.'

She hadn't given him any signals. 'I'd rather forget that.' Evie, feeling horribly awkward, was nevertheless relieved by his surprise apology. Perhaps he wasn't trying to find reasons to fire her. 'How is your finger?'

'Healing.' Carlos flexed his bandaged finger and gave a rueful smile. 'Seriously, Evie. Stay here tonight. It's in the interests of the hotel—you'll get more work done if you're here on the premises.'

What he said made sense.

So why was she hesitating? She'd have somewhere warm to stay and she could start searching for another place tomorrow. 'All right. Thanks. If you're sure.'

'Do you have any dry clothes?'

Evie thought of the bag of belongings she'd left in the basement. 'I have a…a bag downstairs.'

'I'll arrange for someone to collect it. Where did you leave it?'

Flanked by his security team, Rio Zaccarelli left his private jet under the cover of darkness and slid into the waiting car.

'No press—that's good.' Antonio, his senior bodyguard, scanned the area. 'No one knows you're coming. Do you want us to call ahead and warn the hotel? They're expecting you in the afternoon, not at four in the morning.'

'No.' Rio lounged in the back of the car, his eyes hooded as he contemplated the surprise that would no doubt accompany his unexpected arrival. 'I don't want to announce myself.'

Knowing never to question the boss, Antonio simply slammed the car door shut and slid in next to the driver. 'Shouldn't take us long to get there at this hour. No traffic. I suppose it's because it's Christmas. Lots of people have already stopped work.'

Rio didn't reply.

A cold feeling spread across his skin. A feeling that had nothing to do with the dropping temperature and the swirling snowflakes outside the car. He looked out of the window, keeping his expression blank.

Christmas.

Twenty years had passed and yet he still hated this time of year.

If he had his way, Christmas would be scrubbed from the calendar.

Blocking out the endless twinkling lights and Christmas decorations adorning the dark streets, Rio was for once grateful for the endless demands of his BlackBerry.

Anna, the ballerina, had sent him fourteen messages, each one more desperate than the last.

He read the first three, saw the word 'commitment' and deleted the rest without reading them. Christmas, commitment—why was it that his least favourite words all began with C?

The car pulled up outside the hotel and Rio sat for a moment, surveying the elegant architecture. It was the most expensive few acres of real estate in the world.

You'll never make anything of yourself, Rio. You'll amount to nothing.

Rio gave a grim smile as he surveyed 'nothing'.

He owned it. All of it. Every last brick. Not bad for someone who had once watched his life ground into the dirt.

Leaning forward, he spoke to his driver in Italian. 'Take me to the rear entrance.'

'Yes, sir.'

Rio sprang from the car and walked through the rear door of the hotel, his mouth tightening in disapproval as no one challenged him.

Antonio was right behind him. 'I'll go first.'

'No. I want you to go back downstairs and check those security cameras. And time how long it takes them to discover I'm in the building.' Rio sprinted up ten floors and reached the locked door that protected the exclusive Penthouse suite. He entered a code into the pad and the door opened. Realising that no one had changed the code, his mouth tightened and a dangerous spark lit his eyes.

Inside the luxurious suite, it was warm and peaceful.

And decorated for Christmas.

Rio froze.

He'd given strict instructions—no decorations.

His tension levels rocketing, his gaze fastened on the tall fir tree that glittered and sparkled in the elegant living room, taunting him—*reminding him.*

Turning his back on it, he prowled through the suite. His instincts, honed through years of dealing with people, were suddenly on full alert. Something didn't feel right and it wasn't just that his express instructions had been overlooked.

His firm mouth hardened and he walked purposefully towards the bedroom suite, his footsteps muffled by the thick carpet.

Pushing open the door, Rio stopped on the threshold of the room.

Lying on top of the bed was a naked woman, her glorious red hair spilling over the pillow like a spectacular sunset, her eyelashes forming a dark smudge above pale cheeks. Her mouth was a deep pink, her lower lip full and softly curved.

Rio stared at that mouth for a full minute before trailing his gaze down the rest of her body. It wasn't just her mouth that curved. The rest of her did, too, although some of the secrets of her body were concealed beneath all that glorious hair. As he studied the astonishingly vibrant colour, he felt his libido come alive. His mind computed every last detail. Eyes—green, he decided. Temper—hot. Body—*incredible.* She had the longest legs he'd ever seen and, as for the rest of her—

When she didn't stir, he strolled into the room.

Distracted by the full curve of her breasts, he sat down on the edge of the bed and slid a leisurely hand over her shoulder, brushing aside a strand of silky hair.

Unable to resist the sensual curve of her soft mouth, Rio lowered his head and kissed her. He just had time to register that she tasted as good as she looked when her eyes opened.

Deliciously groggy, she stared at him blankly. 'Oh—' Her words were slurred from sleep. 'Is it Christmas?'

If this was Christmas, then maybe it was time he re-evaluated his feelings towards the festive season. Perhaps it wasn't all bad. *Blue,* Rio thought absently, correcting his earlier assumption. Her eyes were the palest aquamarine.

Lust shot through him and he felt himself harden. Because he was staring down at her, he saw the exact moment she was gripped by the same sexual awareness. Those incredible eyes darkened. Her lips parted and he saw the moist tip of her tongue.

Unable to help himself, Rio lowered his head and was about to kiss her again when a light flashed.

He whipped round in time to see a man darting from the room, camera in hand.

Swearing under his breath in Italian, Rio moved with a speed that would have impressed an Olympic sprinter, but the man was already out of the door.

He grabbed his phone from his pocket and speed-dialled his security team but before Antonio could answer the call, Carlos came striding into the room.

'Rio? I was told there was an intruder in the Penthouse. We had no idea you were arriving this early. Reception should have notified me. How was your journey?' He held out his hand in greeting and then froze, his eyes widening as he stared over Rio's shoulder and through the open doors of the bedroom. 'I'm so sorry—I had no idea you had company— how very embarrassing. Rio, forgive me... We'll give you privacy, of course...'

Rio didn't have to look round to identify the reason for the triumphant gleam in the man's eyes. He had his lawyer's words ringing in his ears.

The most important thing is that you need to keep yourself whiter than fresh snow between now and Christmas.

He, of all people, had allowed a woman to distract him and his carelessness could have the most devastating consequences.

He'd been set up.

He'd walked right into a trap.

And now he was going to pay.

CHAPTER TWO

DIZZY from the kiss and fully aware of just how much trouble she was in, Evie scrambled frantically off the bed and then remembered she was naked. She grabbed the silk throw and covered herself, but it refused to co-operate, slipping and slithering through her fingers. Finally she managed to fasten it, sarong-style around her body. She clutched it tightly, praying that it wouldn't fall off. Hurrying through to the living room, she saw Carlos standing there, deep in conversation with a tall, broad-shouldered man. *The man who had kissed her a few moments earlier.*

Still shaken from the explosion of chemistry, a strange heat spread through her body as she took her first proper look at him and immediately her grandfather's words flew into her head—*a real man.*

He dominated the room with the sheer force of his presence, his powerful legs spread apart, his stance unmistakably commanding as he focused furious black eyes on Carlos's face.

Hearing her entrance, he transferred that terrifying gaze to Evie and she stood pinned to the spot, the simmering fury in his eyes acting like a bucket of cold water.

She went from burning to shivering in the space of a glance.

'I...I'd better get dressed,' she stammered and he made a sound in his throat that sounded ominously like a growl.

'You'll stay *exactly* where you are until I give you permission to move.'

Whatever had propelled him to kiss her, it obviously wasn't something he intended to repeat. There was no softness in his eyes. No hint of the sexual promise that had shimmered only moments earlier.

And suddenly she knew exactly who he was and that realisation came with a cold flash of horror. She'd once seen his picture in the back of the hotel brochure—read a statement from the lord and master of the Zaccarelli Leisure Group. The man who had kissed her was Salvatorio Zaccarelli—Rio to the media, who licked their lips over his taste for glamorous women and super-fast cars.

From what she'd read, Evie had already decided that he was a ruthless, cold-hearted money-making machine who didn't give a damn about the human cost of his decisions. When he took a personal interest in one of his hotels the first thing he did was to change everything he didn't like, and that included the staff. He didn't visit when things were going well. Only when they were going badly did he thunder in like an executioner wielding his sword. There was nothing gentle about him. Nothing soft. He treated women the same way as his business. He hired and fired. No one was with him for long.

Evie had planned to keep her head down and stay out of his way.

Realising that her plan had backfired in the most spectacular fashion she stared, terrified, into his smouldering black eyes. He was obviously livid that she'd spent the night in the Penthouse.

Unless Carlos would admit that he'd given her permission, her job was toast.

And so was her dignity.

Evie swallowed hard, wondering why he'd kissed her. From the firm, deliberate seduction of his mouth to the sensuous brush of his hand over her bare skin, it had been a kiss loaded with sizzling chemistry and erotic promise.

Even as she was wondering if it was usual for him to kiss the staff before firing them, a burly man she'd didn't know came sprinting through the door.

'Sorry, boss.' He stared hard at Rio Zaccarelli, as if in some silent communication. 'Lost him. He must have nipped down the back stairs. I've contacted the local police and I'm going to go through the CCTV footage with hotel security. We'll identify him. Do you want me to question the girl?'

Question her? Why would they want to question her? Her crime was straightforward enough, wasn't it?

'You don't know her?' Carlos looked shocked. 'I assumed—why else would she be in your bedroom, Rio?'

Appalled, Evie stared at him. Obviously, Carlos was going to put his own future before hers. Presumably he was worried that if he confessed to having given her permission to sleep in the Penthouse, he'd be disciplined. Feeling intensely vulnerable, she stood there, searching desperately for a way out of this mess.

'Accept my apologies, Rio.' Carlos's voice was smooth. 'We normally screen our staff very carefully but at this time of year when we're so busy—' He left the sentence hanging. 'I'm disappointed in you, Evie. You abused a position of trust.'

'She works here?' Rio Zaccarelli's voice was harsh. 'She's one of your staff?'

Everyone turned to look at her and Evie burned with humiliation. So that was that. No one was going to believe she'd slept in the Penthouse with permission. They'd believe Carlos, not a lowly member of the housekeeping team. She was nothing more than cannon fodder. Whatever happened next, she was doomed.

There was no point in defending herself.

She had no home, no job and it was less than two weeks until Christmas.

Thinking of her grandfather, Evie felt despair seep through her veins. There was no way she could tell him. Not just before Christmas. He was so proud of her new job and the way she'd picked herself up.

You're a real soldier, Evie.

After everything he'd done for her, she'd let him down.

Maybe she should just forget dignity and beg. Or maybe she should try kissing the boss again. Her eyes drifted over his handsome face and rested on his firm, sensuous mouth. *That same mouth that had taken liberties with hers only moments earlier.* Without thinking, she drew her tongue over her lower lip, tasting his kiss.

He saw the gesture and his eyes flared with anger and something else, far, far more dangerous. With a final contemptuous glance, he turned back to Carlos. 'Do you know what you've done?' His voice was thickened with emotion. 'Have you any idea how much damage you've caused?'

Confused, Evie watched as Rio Zaccarelli transferred the full force of his anger onto Carlos. Why? Had he guessed that Carlos had given her permission? Had he seen through the lies? He was rumoured to have a brain as sharp as a blade.

Hope flickered to life inside her. If Rio Zaccarelli knew Carlos had given her permission, then maybe he'd let her off this time.

He had the reputation of being an exacting boss with impossibly high standards, but, all the same—

Sweat shone on Carlos's forehead. 'What damage? I have no idea what you're talking about.'

With a growl of anger, Rio Zaccarelli crossed the room in three long strides and locked his fist in the front of Carlos's shirt. 'Have you no conscience? No sense of human decency?'

Seeing the black expression on Rio Zaccarelli's face, Evie covered her mouth with her hand.

Wasn't he going a bit overboard?

Oh, dear God, he was going to punch creepy Carlos.

And Carlos looked terrified and triumphant at the same time. Although he was undoubtedly afraid, Evie had the strangest feeling that he was enjoying seeing the other man lose control. His expression was mocking rather than apologetic, as if the outcome had exceeded his most extravagant hopes.

Trying to make sense of it and failing, she could do nothing but watch as the drama unfolded in front of her. The two men appeared to have forgotten her existence. They faced each other down like two bulls fighting for territory, but there was no doubt in her mind who was the superior, both in strength and intellect.

While Carlos blustered and bumbled, Rio's anger was cold and a thousand times more frightening.

'If you have lost me this deal—'

'Me?' His voice contradicting the look in his eyes, Carlos sounded shocked. 'You think I had anything to do with this? You seriously think—? Rio, I know you don't need this sort of publicity right now—I know you're at a delicate stage of negotiations. This could ruin everything for you.'

Evie looked on in disbelief, trying to follow the thread of the conversation. This was all about some stupid deal? That was why Ruthless Rio was so angry? What had happened to everyone's priorities? All they thought about was money, money, money.

It was only because she had her eyes fixed on his taut profile that Evie saw the flash of raw emotion cross Rio Zaccarelli's face. For a moment she thought he was going to reach out and grab Carlos by the throat.

Instead, he released him.

'*Vai al diavolo.* Get out of my sight.' His voice was

strangely robotic, his features a mask of contempt. 'From this moment on, I don't know you. You don't work for me and I don't want to hear from you or see you again. Step into one of my hotels and I'll have you removed. My lawyers will sort out the details with you. And if this causes me trouble—if I lose—' He broke off, apparently unable to finish the sentence, his voice thickened with an emotion so much deeper than anger that Evie felt real fear.

How could he be so angry about one stupid deal?

She waited for Carlos to defend himself but the other man shot through the door without looking backwards.

Which, basically, left her alone with a madman.

Evie tightened her grip on the throw. She loathed Carlos, but at least he was a familiar face. If murder was about to be committed, then it might have been useful to have a witness. Or even an alternative victim.

The burly man, who she assumed was a bodyguard, flexed his fingers threateningly. 'Do you want me to deal with him, boss? I reckon I could get the information you want out of him in less than a minute. He's a wimp.'

Another wimp, Evie thought numbly. The world was populated by wimps. Wimps and bullies.

'Don't waste your time.' Rio's tone was ice-cold. 'I know a quicker way of extracting information.'

Realising that she was the 'quicker way', Evie took a step backwards, seriously scared.

'Calm down,' she stammered. 'Take a deep breath—count to ten—or maybe a hundred—' She had absolutely no idea what was going on, but it was obvious that she was in enormous trouble for sleeping in the Penthouse. 'I don't suppose there is any point in saying sorry or trying to explain, but honestly, I don't see that it's that big a deal. I know I did wrong, but I think you're overreacting—' She gulped as Rio Zaccarelli strode towards her.

He stripped off his jacket and threw it over the back of the nearest chair. His white silk shirt moulded to his wide, muscular shoulders, hinting at the power concealed beneath and Evie found herself staring in fascinated horror as he rolled the sleeves back in a deliberate movement. He looked like a boxer preparing for a fight. And she was obviously earmarked as the opponent. She wondered whether he'd removed his screamingly expensive jacket so that he didn't end up with her blood spattered on it.

His eyes dark with fury, he came to a halt right in front of her. 'Not a big deal? Either you are the most insensitive, selfish, greedy woman I've ever met or you have no idea of the magnitude of the trouble you've just caused.'

Up close, she could see the rough shadow that framed his hard jaw. She saw that his eyelashes were thick and dark and that underneath his fierce gaze there were dangerous shadows. Other women talked about his monumental sex appeal, but Evie was too scared to feel anything other than fear. 'I'm not selfish or greedy,' she defended herself in a shaky voice, 'and I honestly don't see that spending a night in that bed is such a big deal. I shouldn't have done it, but I thought the Penthouse was empty overnight. And I didn't even dirty the sheets. I slept on top of the covers.'

'Of course you slept on top of the covers,' he gritted. 'How else could the photographer have taken his picture?' He fisted his hand in the front of the throw and pulled her hard against him. Breathing heavily, the backs of his fingers pressed into her cleavage as he held her trapped.

Evie, who rarely felt intimidated by men because of her height, was definitely intimidated now.

For once she felt dwarfed, his superior height making her feel small and insignificant and she swiftly re-evaluated her belief that it would be nice to meet a man taller than her.

Through the mist of panic, her brain finally latched on to something he'd said.

'Photographer?' Trying to breathe, she stared up at him blankly. 'What photographer?'

His eyes dropped to her mouth and that single look weakened her knees. For a moment she saw what other women saw. Raw sex appeal. She might have been attracted to him herself if she hadn't been so terrified. Wondering if she was the only one who was feeling suffocated, she gasped as he suddenly released her. Her hands shot out to balance herself and the silk throw slid to the ground.

With a squeak of embarrassment, Evie made a grab for it but not before she'd seen the sudden darkening in his eyes and heard the burly security man gulp. 'I need to get dressed!' She'd hung her wet clothes on the heated towel rail in the bathroom, but they ought to be dry by now.

With a contemptuous sound, Rio Zaccarelli turned away from her. 'It's a little late for modesty, don't you think? By tomorrow, that photograph will be all over the world.'

'What photograph?' She wrapped the throw around her as tightly as she could. 'I have no idea what you're talking about.'

Rio gave a growl of anger. 'The photograph of us kissing. I want the name of the photographer and the name of the person who put you up to this. Start giving me facts.'

Evie glanced back towards the bedroom, retracing the events of the past few minutes. 'I...someone took a picture of me?'

A muscle flickered in his jaw. 'Generally, I pride myself on my control but today I seem to be falling short of my usual high standards. If you don't want to see a first-hand demonstration of the meaning of the word angry, then don't play stupid.'

'I'm not playing stupid! I didn't see a photographer. You were in my line of vision, remember? All I saw was you.'

Deep colour highlighted his cheekbones and his eyes

burned. 'Are you seriously expecting me to believe that you didn't see the light or the man running out of the room?'

Evie thought back, but all she could think about was how amazing it had felt to be kissed by him. She remembered warmth, the most incredible excitement, flashing lights— *flashing lights?*

Appalled, she stared at him and his mouth twisted in cynical derision.

'Memory returning?' He was so arrogantly sure of himself that Evie bristled and decided that there was no way she was confessing she'd thought the lights were part of the firework display set off in her body by his incredible kiss. His monumentally overinflated ego obviously didn't need any help from her.

'I didn't see him. As I said, you were blocking my view of the room.'

'Unfortunately, I wasn't blocking his view of you. He now has a picture of us—' his expression was grim as he watched her '—together.'

As the implications of his words sank home, Evie felt her limbs weaken. 'Hold on a moment. Are you telling me that some stranger just took a picture of me, naked on the bed?' Panic and horror rushed up inside her. She hated having her picture taken, even when she was fully clothed, but naked—?

'I've already warned you—I'm not in the mood.' There was no mistaking the deadly warning in his tone or the tension in his body language. He was a man no one was likely to mess with and Evie felt her mouth dry as her gaze clashed with pitch-black eyes.

'I'm not in the mood, either,' she squeaked. 'And I'm not playing games. How did a photographer get in here? Why would he want to take a photograph of me? What's he going to do with it?' Anxiety set her tongue loose but he silenced her with a single searing glance.

'If you utter one more ingenuous question I just might drop you naked on the street outside. How much did he pay you?'

Struggling to keep up with his thought process, Evie opened her mouth and closed it again. 'You honestly think anyone would pay to take a picture of my body? Are you mad?' Her voice rose. 'Presumably, you've already noticed that I'm not exactly a supermodel! The only way anyone would be interested in looking at me naked is one of those hideous before and after photos. You know—*"and this is Evie before she went on the wonder diet and lost twenty kilos."*'

His eyes blazed dark with incredulity. 'Is that all you can think about? Whether the photographer took your good side?'

'No, because I don't have a good side! I look the same from every angle, which is why I never let anyone take my photo!' She'd never before met a man she wanted to kiss and slap at the same time and it was such a shockingly confusing sensation that her head spun. She wanted to defend herself. She wanted to protest that she wasn't superficial and that having a photograph taken of her naked was right up there with her worst nightmares. It was like being back in the playground.

Evie the elephant—

'Wh...what's he going to do with that photograph?' She tried to calm herself down with logic and reason. This wasn't the playground. 'No one is going to want to look at a picture of me naked. There is no reason anyone would want to publish a picture of me...' as she stared into his taut, handsome face, her voice faded to a horrified whisper '...but there's every reason why they'd publish a picture of *you*.' And she was in that picture. Suddenly, everything was clear. She thought of all the vile, degrading 'kiss and tell' stories she'd read. 'Oh, my God—'

Rio was watching her, his mouth tight. 'How much did he pay you?'

'Nothing! I don't know anything about this! I'm as innocent as you are.' But she could tell he didn't believe her and
what she saw in those glittering black eyes was so terrifying
that she wanted to confess everything on the spot. Because
his expression was so scary, she looked at his mouth instead
and suddenly all she was thinking about was that scorching
kiss. *Where had he learned to kiss like that?*

'Innocent girls don't lie in wait, naked, on a guy's bed.'

'I wasn't lying in wait! How could you even think that? I've
been kicked out of my flat and I had nowhere to go last night
and—' Evie thought about the sequence of events. Carlos
had offered her the use of the room. When she'd refused,
he'd insisted. It was Carlos who had encouraged her to take
a shower and dry her wet clothes on the radiator. Appalled,
she looked up at Rio Zaccarelli and saw his mouth tighten
as he read her mind.

'Your face is very revealing, so don't even think of telling
me you have no idea what's going on.' The menacing chill in
his voice confirmed just how much trouble she was in and
she felt the colour drain out of her cheeks as he turned up
the pressure.

'I've been set up.'

A dangerous glint shone in his eyes. 'I'm listening.'

He didn't believe her. 'Carlos gave me instructions to
sleep here tonight—' Evie clutched at the silk throw, her
mind racing forward with possible scenarios, all of which
sickened her. No matter what she said, Rio Zaccarelli wasn't
going to believe that she had nothing to do with this. 'I was
really, really stupid—what are they going to do with that
photograph?'

For a moment he didn't answer. He simply stared at her,
as if he were making a decision about something. A slight
frown touched his brows and he strolled around her, looking at her from the front, the back and the sides. When he
finally spoke, his voice was hard. 'They're going to publish

it. By tomorrow, that photograph will be plastered all over the Internet and the newspapers.'

The bodyguard cleared his throat. 'Boss—'

Rio turned on him and said something in Italian that silenced the other man immediately.

Evie felt faint with horror. *'What?'* That was by far the worst scenario on her list and she gave a low moan of horror as she contemplated exactly what that would mean. 'I thought maybe they'd just use it to blackmail you or something—'

'Is that what they told you?' His tone was dangerously soft. 'Is that what you agreed?'

'No! I didn't agree anything. I was thinking aloud—' Flustered, realising that she was digging herself deeper and deeper into a hole, Evie sank her hand into her hair, trying to think straight so that she could be more articulate. 'What I mean is, at least if it's blackmail they could be persuaded not to publish it. Of all the things they could do with that photo, publishing it would be the worst. Do you have any idea how embarrassing that would be? I'd never be able to go anywhere ever again.'

'Embarrassing? Do you think I care about being embarrassed?' The lethal cocktail of physical height and powerful personality left her shaking and intimidated but all those emotions were eclipsed by the prospect of being exposed physically to the mocking eyes of the world.

'No, you probably don't care—' Evie's voice rose '—because *you're* not the one who was lying there naked with your bottom on full view! And stop trying to scare me! This whole thing is bad enough without having to wonder whether you're going to explode any minute.' She covered her face with her free hand—the other was still clutching the throw, holding it in place. 'Oh, my God—if that photo goes in the papers—everyone I know will see it—Grandpa will see it—he'll be mortified—' Melting with embarrassment, she looked at him helplessly. 'You *have* to do something. You have to stop it.

You're completely loaded—can't you pay them or something? Do whatever it is they want you to do.' The thought of being seen naked in public was the most hideous thing that had ever happened to her. Worse than being demoted. Worse than losing her job. Worse than being dumped by Jeff.

Evie cringed with horror as she tried to work out what angle the flash had come from and remember exactly how she'd been lying.

It took her right back to the nightmare days of hiding in the corner of the girls' changing rooms trying to wriggle into her gym kit with no one noticing.

'If you genuinely care, then perhaps you should have thought of the consequences before you agreed to lie on the bed.'

Evie ground her teeth. 'I lay on the bed because I didn't have anywhere else to lie, OK? I told you—I lost my flat. I was in a fix and when Carlos made that offer—' she licked her lips '—it just seemed too good to be true. Turned out it *was* too good to be true. Look, it doesn't really matter whether you believe me or not. What's important is stopping that photograph. *Please* pay them off.'

His gaze was steady. 'They don't want money.'

'Then what do they want?'

He turned away from her but not before she'd seen the dark shadow flicker across his face. 'They want to make my life…difficult.'

'What about *my* life?'

'They're not interested in you. You've played your part. You're expendable. I'm sure you can find some lucrative way to use your five minutes of fame.'

'Do you honestly think I want to be famous for the size of my bottom?'

'If you are genuinely distressed about the idea of being pictured, why did you agree to this?'

'Are you thick or something? *I didn't agree to it!*'

There was a crashing sound as the door to the suite burst open behind him and three uniformed hotel security men pounded into the room, horribly out of breath.

Evie suddenly wished she could vanish into thin air.

Rio took a slow, deliberate look at the watch on his wrist. 'I have been in this hotel for seventeen minutes,' he said in an icy tone, 'and no one has challenged me. That is sixteen and a half minutes too long. The security code for the Penthouse hasn't been changed since the last time I stayed here as a guest, which is presumably how a complete stranger managed to access the suite. The security camera at the rear entrance is pointed away from the street. A journalist managed to get access to my suite. Is this how you protect the guests in your care?'

Evie watched as Arnold's forehead grew shiny with sweat. The security chief was one of the few people who had been kind to her since she'd arrived in London and she felt a tiny flame of anger warm her insides as she saw him squirm.

'We didn't know you were arriving in the middle of the night, sir. We were expecting you later this morning and—' His jaw dropped as he saw Evie. '*Evie?* What are you doing in the Penthouse?'

Evie tightened her grip on the silk bedspread. 'I had nowhere to sleep last night, Arnold—'

Rio's eyes narrowed. 'You know this woman?'

'Of course. Her name is Evie Anderson.' Arnold's expression softened. 'She works here as a receptionist—I mean, a member of the housekeeping staff.'

Evie was just beginning to hope that Arnold might vouch for her integrity when the door to the Penthouse opened again and a portly woman in her fifties arrived, breathless and flustered. It was obvious that she'd dressed in a hurry and her skirt was on back to front and the buttons on her shirt unaligned. Clearly woken from sleep, one half of her hair was flattened to her head and the other was in wild disarray.

Evie groaned in horror. *No.* How had Tina found out?

'Mr Zaccarelli—we were expecting you much later to-day—I'm so sorry no one was here to greet you—' Oozing deference, the woman's discomfiture was almost painful to watch. 'I'm Tina Hunter, Director of Guest Relations. We're going to do anything in our power to make sure your stay here is memorable.'

Tina's eyes widened with horror as she turned her head and saw Evie.

'Evelyn? What do you think you're doing?' She turned back to Rio, squirming with mortification. 'I'm *so* sorry. She's given us nothing but trouble, that girl—thinks she's better than the rest of us. It's my fault for giving her a second chance, but that's me all over. I've always been a soft touch. Evelyn, I want you to collect your things and go.'

Shocked by the injustice, Evie stared at her. 'You haven't even asked for my side of the story.'

Tina's cheeks turned scarlet. 'You're naked in a guest's bedroom. That's enough for me. Let me just say that I find it incredibly tacky that you would try and force yourself on a billionaire.'

'Excuse me?' Almost speechless with outrage, Evie exploded. 'Look at the guy! Even if I wanted to, I'm hardly likely to be able to force myself on him, am I? He's built like a—' Her voice tailed off and colour poured into her cheeks.

Tina was shaking with anger. 'Get your things.'

'I don't have any things. Everything I owned was in a bag and I left it in the basement. Carlos was supposed to arrange for it to be brought up here so that I could change into dry clothes. Funnily enough, it never appeared.' Evie scraped a strand of hair behind her ear with a hand that shook, afraid that this was going to be the moment that she finally lost it.

She felt tears scald the back of her eyes as she made a last-ditch attempt to extricate herself. 'Carlos ordered me to sleep here last night, not that I expect any of you to believe me.'

'Of course we don't believe you!' Tina exploded. 'Why would the Manager of this hotel give a member of the house-keeping staff permission to spend the night in the Penthouse? A room that costs twelve thousand pounds a night.'

Evie paled. 'How much? That's outrageous.'

'What's outrageous is you standing there behaving like Lady Godiva. You need to find yourself another job, young lady. Since you're so free with your body, I'm sure there are no end of options open to you if you're seeking new employment,' Tina snapped. 'And don't look so shocked. You're standing there half naked, so this "I'm an innocent girl from the country" act is wearing a little thin. You may look wholesome, but I think we all know different. Why do you think I moved you off Reception? We had such a crowd around the desk, the hotel almost ground to a standstill.'

'I was being friendly! You told me I was the public face of the hotel and I assumed you'd want that face to be smiling, not miserable! You're *so* unfair—it's Christmas and there's not a single drop of Christmas spirit or compassion in any of you. And I'm naked because my clothes were wet, not because I want a career as a porn star.'

Tina pointed towards the door. 'You're fired. Get out.'

'What, dressed like this?' Evie gaped at her. 'No way! This is the throw from the bed and I'm not giving you reason to sue me for theft on top of everything else, not to mention indecent exposure as I trail along the corridors. I think you're all vile. None of this is my fault, but I'm going to be the one who suffers. I'll get dressed and then I'll leave and I hope you all have a really Happy Christmas!' Thinking of her grandfather's reaction when he saw the photograph of her naked and kissing a stranger, Evie gave a strangled moan and shot into the only room with a lock on the door.

* * *

Wholesome—

Rio stared at the locked door, his mind moving faster than the speed of sound as he swiftly formulated a plan that could turn this situation to his advantage.

Square-jawed, purple in the face, Tina turned to the security men with the purpose of an army commander preparing for a forward push. 'She's locked herself in. Open that door and escort her off the premises. We'll do what we can to keep this out of the papers.'

Rio roused himself. Fired by the challenge, always at his best under pressure, he took control.

'Out,' he ordered harshly, striding towards the door of the suite and holding it open. 'All of you. Now.'

They all looked at each other and Rio gave a smile that shifted the atmosphere from one of tension to one of terror.

'Organise a staff meeting for one o'clock this afternoon.' Like a laser-guided weapon locking on his target, he transferred his gaze to the security chief. 'At that meeting I want the name of the person responsible for the fact that the security cameras in the street were pointing the wrong way. I want a report on how security at the hotel can be upgraded so that I have a guarantee that any intruder entering this building will be challenged within thirty seconds of entering the premises—'

'But this is a hotel, sir; people come and go—'

'If you're not up to the job, just say so, and I'll replace you with someone who is. My personal security team will assist you in preparing the report, if you wish to stay.'

Arnold quailed under that icy stare and Rio continued.

'It's your job to differentiate between guest, gawker and criminal. That's the job I pay you to perform. And you—' Rio shifted his gaze to Tina. 'You're fired.'

Tina gaped at him, her jaw slack, her unmade-up face an unflattering shade of scarlet. 'You can't just fire me—'

'I own this hotel. I can do anything I like.'

'You have no grounds—'

'Bullying and staff intimidation are grounds enough in my book,' Rio said coldly, 'and that's just the beginning. I have a full report on my desk, which includes recommendations on staffing. Your name appears on almost every page. Do you want me to go on?'

Tina gulped and opened her mouth but no sound came out.

Without a flicker of expression on his face, Rio opened the door wider. 'That's it,' he said pleasantly. 'You can go now. And on your way out ask someone to come and remove this Christmas tree. While I'm staying here, I don't want to know it's Christmas. Am I understood? No baubles, no berries, no tree, no tinsel.'

One by one, they shot past him and Tina paused, clearly panicking about her future. 'What about Evelyn? She's the cause of all this. She should be removed from the premises.'

Rio, who had been rapidly formulating a backup strategy since 'whiter than white' had exploded into the ether, sent her a look that had her scurrying out of the door.

Strolling back to the bathroom, he stared with brooding concentration at the closed door.

Wholesome.

The problem might just turn out to be the solution, he mused.

'All right, Sleeping Beauty. I've slain your dragon. You can come out now.'

CHAPTER THREE

He'd fired Tina!

With her ear pressed to the smooth wood of the door, Evie listened with her mouth open, unable to believe what she was hearing.

Afraid to make a sound in case he realised she'd been eavesdropping, she tiptoed away from the door and leaned her burning cheek against the cool marble wall of the bathroom, her knees weak and shaking.

He'd seen right through Tina and fired her on the spot. Obviously, the rumours about him being super-bright were true. All right, so he was ruthless and wasn't afraid to axe jobs, but still—maybe he wasn't so bad...

Still in shock, Evie let out a long breath. She felt as though she should feel sorry for Tina, but it was hard to feel sorry for someone who created an atmosphere of intimidation. She remembered the threats, both spoken and unspoken, the way she transformed confident staff into doubting, apologetic wrecks. Since her demotion to housekeeping, Evie had mopped up more tears than she had floors.

Had he heard the rumours? Was that what he'd meant by seeing Tina's name on every page of his report?

Who else was on his list to be fired?

Realising that she had to be right at the top, Evie closed her eyes.

There was no doubt in her mind that she was going to be next and she didn't even care any more. All she cared about was that stupid, horrid photograph. Perhaps she ought to ring Cedar Court and ask the staff to make sure that her grandfather didn't see any newspapers or television.

But her grandfather loved his newspaper. He did the crossword every day.

If they banned it, he'd just want to know why.

Hyperventilating again, Evie clutched the edge of the washbasin and forced herself to breathe steadily.

She'd thought life couldn't get much worse, but suddenly it was a million times more disastrous.

Her grandfather would panic if he knew she'd lost her job and had nowhere to live, but it was nothing to what he'd do when he saw pictures of her naked and kissing a stranger. She could just imagine what Mrs Fitzwilliam would make of that. *I hear your precious little Evie has turned into a bit of a goer—*

'You have ten seconds to come out of that bathroom.'

The deep male voice held sufficient authority to confirm all Evie's darkest suspicions about his intentions. He was obviously dealing with his problems with the brutal efficiency for which he was famed, and she was the next problem on his list. *The worst was still to come.*

She looked round desperately, searching for an escape. Apart from flushing herself down the toilet or trying to squeeze down the plughole, there was no way out of this bathroom.

Why, oh, why, had she taken up creepy Carlos's suggestion of sleeping in the Penthouse? Why hadn't she followed her initial instinct that it was a bad idea? And why had Rio Zaccarelli decided to arrive at the hotel early when the rest of London was asleep? The man obviously was a machine.

'Two seconds—' The hard, cold voice made her jump and Evie stared helplessly at the door, trying to think what to do.

She needed a plan. She needed to think what she could say that might help her situation.

While she was in here, she was safe. What could he do? He was hardly going to break the door down, was he?

There was a tremendous crash, the sound of wood splintering and Evie screamed as the door crashed open, slamming against the sleek limestone wall of the luxurious bathroom.

Rio Zaccarelli stood in the doorway rubbing his shoulder. 'What is the matter with the staff in this place? When I give you an order,' he thundered, 'I expect you to follow it. And I *don't* expect to have to demolish my hotel so that I can hold a conversation with one of my employees.'

Stunned that the door was still on its hinges, Evie gulped. 'I—you—are you *OK*? I mean—I've seen people crash through doors in the movies but I always assumed the door is made out of cardboard or something. I've never seen anyone actually do it with a real door. That must have hurt.' She looked at his powerful shoulders doubtfully, wondering whether all that muscle would act as a barrier to pain.

'*Sì,* it hurt.' He rolled his shoulder experimentally, checking for damage. 'Which is why, next time, I'd appreciate it if you'd just do as I say and open the damn door.'

Evie gave a choked laugh, clutching the silk throw against her. 'Why? So that you can fire me in person?'

'Who says I'm going to fire you?'

'You fired the tyrannosaurus.'

'Tyrannosaurus?' Still rubbing his shoulder, he frowned, his expression dark and menacing. 'I presume you're talking about that officious woman with the unfortunate hair. That's what you all call her?'

Evie froze. 'No, of course not,' she lied. 'We call her Tina.' *Or meat-eater, because she feasted on hotel staff for breakfast.*

'She didn't seem too impressed with you.'

'No.' It was impossible to argue with that. Utterly defeated,

Evie felt the last dregs of spirit drain out of her. What was the point in defending herself? It was over. 'I think it's fair to say I don't have an enormous number of supporters in high places.' Tina had demoted her. Carlos had tried to grope her and, when she'd rejected him and humiliated him, he'd set her up.

Thinking of her grandfather, Evie wondered whether it was worth begging Rio Zaccarelli to give her another chance. Gazing into those unsympathetic black eyes, she decided that it was a waste of breath. She doubted there was a gram of compassion anywhere in his muscle-packed frame.

'I have a big problem.' His deep voice slid over her nerve-endings like treacle and Evie snatched in a breath, shocked by the sudden heat that shot through her. Underneath the dangerously slippery silk throw, she was suddenly horribly conscious that she was still naked.

If ever there was a more uneven confrontation, this had to be it.

Everything about him suggested raw masculine power, from the dusky shadow of his jaw to the tiny scar that flawed the skin above his right eye.

A vision of Jeff's baby-smooth face flew into her head but Evie realised that to make comparisons between the two men would be nothing short of ridiculous. They had nothing in common. Nothing at all.

Rio Zaccarelli might have been dressed for a formal dinner, but the external trappings of sophistication didn't fool her for a moment. This man wasn't tame or civilised. He was hard and unyielding and he'd do whatever he needed to do to achieve what he wanted.

A real man.

Suffocated by the heat in the air, her limbs suddenly felt heavy and her heart hammered against her ribs. Her instincts were telling her to run, but she couldn't move.

She tried to conjure up an image of Jeff's face again but

found that she couldn't. Instead, her mind was filled with a vision of burnished skin and eyes full of sexual promise.

To make matters worse, two walls of the opulent bathroom were mirrored, which meant that his iron-hard physique was reproduced several times over, dominating her vision.

Seriously unsettled, Evie clutched at the throw. 'If you'd give me five minutes privacy, I'll get dressed.'

'You own clothes?'

'Of course I own clothes! They're drying on the—' Evie turned her head and her eyes widened. 'I left them right there—on the radiator. They're gone.' Her mind explored possible explanations and came up with only one. Feeling the panic rise again, she looked at him and he lifted an eyebrow in weary mockery.

'They walked out of the room under their own steam?'

'Forget it.' Her voice choked, Evie lifted her hand like a stop sign. 'I've had enough of this! There's no point in me saying anything because you're not going to believe me anyway.'

'Strangely enough, you're wrong.' His tone was grim. 'I'm guessing that Carlos had something to do with the mysterious disappearance of your clothes. Am I right?'

Evie lowered her hand slowly. 'H-how do you know that?'

'Because he invited you to stay in the Penthouse and I doubt he did that out of generosity of spirit.'

Relief spurted through her veins. 'I didn't think you believed me—'

'I never thought you acted alone. Now it's all slotting together—' A muscle flickered in his cheek and he muttered something in Italian under his breath.

Evie was rigid with tension. 'I didn't know what was going on. I still don't, but it doesn't really matter. I just want to get out of here. If someone could lend me some clothes, I can go.'

'You're not going anywhere.'

Her heart rate increased. 'If that whole naked photograph thing was a set up then the best thing is surely for me to get as far away from here as possible. I'll go somewhere no one can find me.'

He started to laugh, but there was no trace of humour in the rich masculine sound. It was loaded with cynicism and derision. 'Are you really that naive? The press can find anyone.'

That news shook Evie. 'But why would they want to? I'm no one.'

'Perhaps you were "no one" before you chose to lie naked on my bed with me, but now you're a person of extreme interest.'

'I wasn't *with* you.'

'Yes, you were.'

'Well, that part was your fault. You were the one who kissed me and, quite frankly, I have no idea why you did that.' And she wished he hadn't because, in the midst of this crisis, those feelings kept rushing back to torture her.

His mouth, moving over hers with erotic purpose.

'None of this is my responsibility. You were the one lying there naked.' He issued that statement with such arrogance that Evie simply gaped at him, wondering how it was possible to be terrified of someone and turned on at the same time.

'And that means what? That you kiss every naked woman you see?'

'Normally, the woman gets naked *after* I kiss her,' he drawled. 'That's the usual order of things. Despite the lengths some women go to attract my attention, no one has ever gone quite as far as stripping naked and lying on my bed. That was a first.'

'I thought we'd established that I was set up!' Evie's voice rose. 'If I'd known you were going to arrive early, do you honestly think I would have been lying there?'

'Yes. That photograph will sell for a fortune.'

'Maybe it will, but it won't be me making the fortune,' Evie snapped, stalking out of the bathroom with the throw trailing behind her like a wedding gown.

'Where do you think you're going?'

'Out of here. I'm sick of seeing your reflection in the mirrors. One of you is bad enough. Ten is more than I can take. I'm going to ring Housekeeping and get them to send up a uniform and then I'm going to go and hide somewhere even the press can't find me.'

'Running is *not* the way to handle this.'

'Well, if you can think of a different plan, I'd love to hear it. This is easy for you. You have bodyguards and you own tall buildings with fancy security. All you have to do is lock yourself in your gilded palace until the fuss dies down, but I have to live with the fact that photograph is out there. Everyone who wants a laugh can look at it. They'll probably start a Facebook page for it—*The biggest bottom in the world.*' Evie tripped on the throw and stumbled. Steadying herself, she blinked back tears. 'I have to live with the fact that my eighty-six-year-old grandfather is going to see me with my naked bottom in the air, kissing a stranger! If he has another one of his turns it will be *all* your fault.'

'Which is going to shock him most? Seeing your naked bottom, or the fact that you're kissing a stranger?'

Evie snatched the phone up. 'You're not even funny.'

'Do I look as though I'm laughing? You have *no idea* how serious this is for me. For you, it's embarrassing; for me, it's—' He broke off, his voice unsteady and Evie paused with the handset in her hand, transfixed by the raw emotion she saw in his eyes.

'For you it's what? A deal you don't want to lose? Is this an ego thing? It has to be because you clearly don't care about the embarrassment and I can't honestly believe you'd be making this much fuss about money. I mean, it's not as if you don't already have plenty!' When he didn't answer, she gave a humourless laugh. 'Oh, forget it. I don't know why I'm expecting you to care any more than Carlos cared. Why does it matter to you that one more woman's reputation is shattered? I'm just another notch on your bedpost.'

'I do not make notches on my bedpost,' he said thickly. 'I am very choosy about my relationships.'

And he wouldn't be choosing a woman like her. Evie turned scarlet and stabbed the number for Housekeeping. 'Hello? Margaret? I'm really sorry to bother you, but could you possibly deliver a fresh housekeeping uniform to the Penthouse, please. I've…spilled something…sorry?' She blushed and turned her head away, lowering her voice. 'Size twelve…I said size twelve…I'm not whispering—' She gave a gasp as the phone was removed from her fingers.

'She said size twelve,' Rio drawled, 'and, while you're at it, send some underwear and shoes. She takes a—' his gaze slid to her cleavage '—thirty-four DD and her feet are—' He lifted an eyebrow in Evie's direction.

'Forty,' she said faintly and he delivered that information in the same commanding tone and ended the call. Then he answered his mobile, which was buzzing in his pocket and spoke at length in Italian, leaving Evie standing with a scarlet face, still trying to work out how he'd been able to guess her bra size so accurately.

He was still in mid-conversation when there was another buzzing sound and he drew his BlackBerry out of a different pocket without breaking conversation.

Evie watched in disbelief as he talked into one phone while emailing from the other.

'*Sì—Sì—Ciao.*' He ended the conversation and frowned at her. 'Why are you staring?'

'How many phones do you have?'

'Three. It makes me more efficient.'

'What happens if they ring at the same time? Most men aren't that good at multi-tasking.'

He gave a cool smile. 'I'm not most men. And I'm excellent at multi-tasking.' As if to test that theory, two of his three phones rang simultaneously and Evie moved to the window as he dealt swiftly with one call and then the other.

It was still dark outside, but the roads far beneath her were already busy as cars and taxis inched their way over snowy streets.

She leaned her cheek against the glass, watching people carrying on with their lives, wishing she could swap with them. Or put the clock back. She wished she'd never spent the night in the Penthouse.

Her eyes stung with tears and she blinked rapidly, determined not to cry. It was just because she was tired, she told herself fiercely.

What should she do? She couldn't decide whether it was better to ring her grandfather and warn him that he might see some very embarrassing pictures of her in the press, or say nothing and just hope that he didn't read that page in the paper.

But someone was bound to point it out, weren't they? She never ceased to be depressed by the enjoyment some people took from watching another's misfortune.

'Move away from the windows. Your clothes have arrived—you can change in the bedroom.'

Evie turned, wondering how her colleagues in Housekeeping had managed to produce underwear and shoes so quickly. Then she looked at the elegant packaging on the boxes and realised they'd simply used the expensive store in the hotel foyer.

'I can't afford to pay for those.'

He looked at her with ill-disguised impatience. 'The price tag on your bra is surely the least of our worries at the moment.'

'To you, maybe, but that's because you don't have to worry about money,' Evie said stubbornly. 'I do. Particularly as I appear to have just lost my job.'

The phone rang in his pocket again but this time he ignored it. 'Get dressed. Consider the clothes a gift.'

'I can't accept a gift of underwear from you. It wouldn't be right.'

'In that case, think of them as an essential part of our crisis management programme. The longer you continue to walk around naked, the more likely we are to find ourselves in even hotter water.'

He had a point.

Opening one of the boxes, Evie spotted a silky leopard-print bra and panties and crushed the lid back down, her face scarlet. 'I can't wear something like that.' Hardly daring to look, she prised the lid off the other box and her eyes widened when she saw the contents. 'I can't wear those, either—'

'Why not? They're shoes. I realize they're not strictly uniform, but they will do until we can get you something else.'

'But—' She stared down at the sexy shoe with the wicked heel. It was the most beautiful, extravagant, indulgent thing she'd ever seen. 'I don't wear heels. I can't.'

'You don't have to walk far in them.'

'It isn't the walking.' Her face was almost the same shade of scarlet as the sole of the famous shoes. 'You may not have noticed, but I'm already taller than the average woman. If I wear heels, I look like a freak. Everyone will stare.'

'After last night, they're going to be staring anyway. They'll stare harder and longer if you're barefoot. Put them on.' Without giving her the opportunity to argue, he turned back to the phone, leaving Evie to stare at him in exasperation, wondering what day it was. Had December nineteenth been designated Humiliate Evie Day and someone had forgotten to tell her?

Juggling the throw with the boxes, she struggled into the master bedroom and closed the doors. At least she wouldn't be naked.

Feeling relieved to finally ditch the throw, Evie slung it back on the bed and slithered into the underwear. It fitted perfectly. Then she pushed her feet into the shoes, almost losing her balance as she teetered precariously on the vertiginous heels. She felt like a circus performer practising on stilts.

Risking a look in the mirror, she gave a moan of horror.

She *looked* like a circus performer.

She looked like a giant.

She was about to take them off when the door to the bedroom opened.

Rio's gaze swept her from head to foot.

'*Maledizione*—' His eyes went dark with shock and Evie wanted to fall through the floor as she intercepted his look of stunned astonishment.

Embarrassment got her moving. 'Get out,' she shrieked, grabbing the throw again. 'I'm getting changed.'

'Does the phrase "shutting the stable door after the horse has bolted" mean anything to you? I've already seen you naked.' Displaying not the slightest consideration for her feelings, he allowed his gaze to travel slowly down every centimetre of her body. 'I've never seen a woman who looks like you.'

For Evie, already sensitive about her looks, his comment delivered the final blow to her crumbling self-esteem.

'It's your fault for getting me those stupid shoes when anyone with half a brain could have guessed they'd make me look ridiculous. And that's before I put on the uniform. I always wear flats, OK? Ballet pumps. Court shoes with no heel. Get out of here! I'm fed up with being a laughing stock, although I suppose I ought to get used to it because it's nothing to how I'm going to feel tomorrow when that photo is published—' Pushed to the limit, she flopped onto the bed, buried her face in the pillow and sobbed her heart out.

Everyone was going to see her naked and her grandfather was going to be horribly, hideously ashamed of her. She'd wanted to make him proud, but the truth was all he really wanted was to bounce a great-grandchild on his knee and that was never going to happen.

She was a big, fat disappointment.

Lost in the nightmare of the moment, she gasped in shock as strong hands closed over her shoulders and Rio flipped her onto her back.

'Stop crying!' He sounded exasperated. 'You'll make your eyes red and that could ruin everything.'

'Ruin what? Just go away. Stop mocking me.'

Astonishment lit his dark eyes. 'When have I ever mocked you?'

'You said you'd never seen anyone who l-looked like me,' Evie hiccuped, 'and I think it's horribly mean of you to poke fun of me, even if it is partly my fault we're in this mess. We're not all supermodels and wearing supermodel labels doesn't change that. I can push my feet into designer shoes just like Kate Moss but that doesn't give me Kate Moss's legs.'

'Which is a good thing,' he drawled, 'because Kate would find it extremely hard to strut her stuff on the runway if you had her legs. For the record, I wasn't mocking you. I was complimenting you.'

Evie, who had never been complimented on her looks in her life before, looked at him through eyelashes welded together with tears. 'Pardon?'

His jaw tensed. 'I find you attractive. Why the hell do you think I kissed you in the first place?'

'Because you have an abnormal sex drive and you can't resist anyone naked?'

'I have a healthy sex drive.' His dark gaze was unmistakably sexual. 'I *definitely* don't kiss women who try and pick me up. That's a first for me.'

'I wasn't trying to pick you up—' Still struggling to accept the unlikely fact that he actually did find her attractive, Evie sat up. 'You don't think I'm too tall?'

'Too tall for what?' That silky tone turned her insides into a quivering mass.

'For…a woman.' Evie licked her lips. 'I make most men feel small and insignificant. They usually don't want to stand next to me. But I guess you're pretty tall yourself.'

'Six four,' he breathed, his eyes scanning the length of her legs. 'And I've never had a problem with a woman's height.'

That was because he was unlikely to meet a woman taller than him, Evie thought weakly. 'Most people think I'm a freak.'

Without giving her a chance to argue, he scooped her off the bed and dumped her on her feet in front of the mirror. 'Look at yourself. Tell me what you see.'

Evie closed her eyes. 'I don't see anything.'

'Look!'

Evie flinched and opened one eye cautiously. 'Evie the elephant,' she said immediately and his brows met in an impatient frown.

'If that title is a throwback to your childhood, then you'd better let it go now. You're stunning and that gives us a major problem.'

Stunning?

Evie, who couldn't even for a single moment think why being considered stunning would present a major problem to anyone, looked at him dizzily. 'Even if that was true, which it isn't, I don't see how that could be a problem. How can being stunning be a problem? People judge by appearances. I've never been a member of the "oh, it's such a bore to be beautiful" camp.'

'It's a problem because you need to look wholesome.'

Evie was about to say that she'd been trying to escape from the 'wholesome' image for most of her life, when he took her hair in his hands and twisted it, assessing the effect with narrowed eyes. 'You have good skin.'

'And freckles.'

'Freckles are good. They suggest a healthy outdoor life. Wholesome.'

Why did he keep saying wholesome?

'I'm not with you—'

'Unfortunately, you *are* with me and that is why we have a problem.'

'We wouldn't have a problem if you hadn't kissed me.'

'I'm fully aware of that fact.' He paced over to the window, keeping his back to her. 'Get dressed.'

Wriggling into the housekeeper uniform, Evie stared at his broad shoulders. 'I don't understand why you're so stressed about this. You celebrities are always in the newspapers. You may be the reason they want that photo, but it's going to damage me far more than you.'

He turned, and the expression on his face was all it took to silence her. His eyes were haunted and there was a tension in his body that was unmistakably real.

'The damage to me could be incalculable,' he said coldly and Evie thought back to the exchange he'd had earlier with Carlos.

Whatever the 'deal' was, he was obviously prepared to stop at nothing to make sure it went through. It had to be about more than money, she thought. It had to be something to do with ego. Winning. The addictive quality of power.

'And creepy Carlos did this to you on purpose and I got caught in the middle, is that right?'

'So it would seem.'

She wondered what Carlos had against Rio Zaccarelli. What was he trying to achieve with that photograph? If it hadn't been her, would he have used someone else? 'If there is no way you can stop that photograph being published then I'd better make a phone call.'

His eyes narrowed. 'You're calling a lover?'

Evie gave a hysterical laugh. 'Oh, yes—I have loads of those—' Catching the dangerous gleam in his eyes, her laughter faded. 'Not a lover. I'm calling my grandfather, if you must know.'

Bold black eyebrows met in a fierce frown. 'How old are you?'

'Twenty-three, but, like most people of his generation, he doesn't believe in public displays of affection,' Evie said wearily, 'and he absolutely doesn't believe in one-night stands. Neither do I, for that matter.' She tried to sound casual, as if talking about sex was something she did all the time, rather than something she never did.

She stared at Rio Zaccarelli, the epitome of male sophistication, and felt her face grow scarlet.

Her grandfather definitely would have classed him as a real man.

It was the ultimate irony, she thought, to have been caught naked with him.

As if—

'So you don't have a lover at the moment.' His slumberous gaze rested on her mouth. 'That's good.'

'Well, that depends on where you're standing,' Evie muttered, wishing she wasn't standing quite so close to him. She was getting hotter and hotter. 'If you must know, I was supposed to be getting married yesterday but my fiancé dumped me. If that hadn't happened I'd be in Bali now, not London. I wouldn't have lost my job and my flat and generally had a completely awful six weeks and there might have been the smallest, remotest chance that my grandfather might be bouncing a baby on his knee next Christmas. As it is, there's no chance. None. I don't expect you to understand. You look like the sort of person whose life always goes according to plan.'

'My plan,' he said tightly, 'wasn't to find a strange woman lying naked in my bed. Fortunately, I've always considered adaptability to be an asset. I can turn this situation around.'

'You can?' Evie's gaze drifted to the neck of his shirt. Dark hairs tangled at the base of his throat and disappeared inside the snowy-white shirt. She imagined the hair hazing his chest and narrowing over his abdomen, which was no doubt as muscular as the rest of him. Shocked by her own thoughts, she lifted her eyes back to his and discovered that he was watching her with an unsettling degree of sexual interest.

'*Why* did he dump you?'

'Why does it matter?' *Was she supposed to read him a list?* Evie chewed the corner of her fingernail and then gave an embarrassed shrug. 'Because he met someone more exciting. Because I'm the girl next door and he's known me since I was three years old. Because I was taller than him and I made him feel less of a man—' She stared at him with exasperation, wondering why she was having to spell this out. 'Because I'm *me*. He sent me a text, dumping me.'

His lips thinned with disapproval. 'That's bad.'

'Hypocrite. Are you seriously trying to tell me you've never dumped a woman?'

'I wouldn't use the word "dumped". I've ended plenty of relationships, but always in person. I've never sent a text. That's cowardly.'

'I suppose it's human nature to avoid a difficult conversation.'

'Difficult conversations are part of my daily existence.'

Evie had no trouble believing that. 'Jeff is nothing like you.' A wimp, her grandfather had called him. 'Perhaps he was sensible. After all the lies he told, I would have blacked his eye if he'd told me in person.'

His eyes lingered on her hair. 'A true redhead with a temper to match.'

Reminded of the embarrassing fact that he knew she was a true redhead, Evie ploughed on. 'What this boils down to is that my grandfather isn't going to be impressed to see me naked with another man. He's very old-fashioned. I don't want him to think I'm like that. I'm *not* like that! I don't flit from one man to another.'

'Unless the other man was someone important to you.' Rio spoke under his breath and she had a feeling that he was thinking aloud.

That thought was confirmed when she muttered, 'Sorry?' and received no response.

'If it was someone you'd been secretly seeing. A rebound relationship that turned into something special—' He paced the length of the bedroom and then turned to look at her, his eyes burning dark. 'Wholesome.'

'You make me sound like a breakfast cereal,' she said irritably. 'Why do you keep saying that?'

'Never mind. How long ago did you start working here?'

'I don't know...I...'

'Think!'

'Don't shout at me! I can't concentrate when people shout!'

Rio sucked in a breath. 'I'm *not* shouting. I just want an answer. When?'

'About six weeks ago. I came down after Jeff dumped me. I started as a receptionist. I thought it was my big break.'

'Six weeks—' Before the words had left his lips, his BlackBerry was in his hand and he was checking something. 'I was staying in the Penthouse six weeks ago. I spent one night here on my way to New York. I need you to find out if you were working here then.'

'I know I was because I made a point of avoiding you. So

what? What difference does that make?' Failing to follow his train of thought, Evie looked at him blankly but he was already dialling a number and speaking into his phone in Italian.

He made call after call and each time Evie opened her mouth to ask him what was going on, he simply lifted his hand to silence her until she was ready to scream with exasperation.

'Hello, I'm here too!' After his seventh consecutive phone call, she waved at him. 'I need to ring my grandfather.'

'First, I want to get this announcement into the press and arrange a photo.'

'What announcement? What photo?' Worried, irritable, Evie snapped at him. 'Haven't we had enough photos for one day?'

He gave a lethal smile. 'This photograph will be different.'

'Different as in I get to wear clothes? Yippee.' She didn't know how she was still managing to joke because she'd never felt less like joking about anything in her life.

She knew enough about the press to understand that scandal and humiliation sold better than anything else. 'Can't you just stop them printing the photograph? Isn't there a privacy law or something?'

'That isn't going to help us. The best thing we can do is stop this whole thing looking sleazy.' Ruthlessly focused, he strode towards the door of the Penthouse. 'Stay out of sight. Whatever you do, don't emerge from the bedroom until I come and get you. I don't want anyone to see you.'

'Why? What are you going to do?'

'Find you some proper clothes and then show the world we didn't have a one-night stand.'

Bemused, Evie stared at him. 'How?'

'By proving that we share something special.' A triumphant gleam in his eyes, he yanked open the door and turned to look at her. 'I'm going to announce our engagement.'

CHAPTER FOUR

Rio gave his Director of Communications a volley of instructions over the phone and then updated his lawyers.

Listening to Pietro's dire predictions, he felt his stomach clench.

Whiter than white....

He should have anticipated this.

He should have known they'd do something to try and stop this deal going through. He'd been arrogant, allowing himself to relax and think that the whole thing was in the bag.

Sweat cooled his brow and he realised that his hand was shaking. Making a conscious effort to control his breathing, he hauled his emotions back and buried them deep. Emotions had no place in negotiation, he knew that. And this was the most complex, delicate negotiation he'd ever conducted.

'Whatever it takes,' he promised his lawyer. 'You wanted wholesome—I'm giving you wholesome.'

When the delivery arrived at the Penthouse, he dismissed the staff member and took the boxes through to the bedroom himself. He then handed them to the girl without breaking off his conversation and without risking another look at her luxuriant red hair.

Why the hell had he kissed her?

He was well aware that his own libido had catapulted him into this situation. If he'd taken one look at her and left the room, the photographer wouldn't have been able to get his shot.

As it was…

With a low growl, Rio focused his mind on the present.

Having hammered out the plan with his team in Rome, he was about to call his team in New York when he heard the bedroom door open.

The girl stood there, her eyes blazing with anger, her hair flowing like liquid fire down her back. 'Excuse me! In case you've forgotten, this affects me, too. Do you intend to discuss any of this with me or are you just going to do your own thing?'

'I don't problem solve by committee.' Congratulating himself on his brief to the stylist, Rio scanned the discreet, elegant dress with satisfaction. It was perfect. She managed to look wholesome and sexy at the same time. *This could just work.* 'I'm busy sorting out our problem right now.'

'No, Mr Zaccarelli, you're sorting out *your* problem—I'm incidental. You haven't once asked what I want to do about this mess which, by the way, is ultimately the fault of you and your stupid, slimy hotel manager, who can't keep his hands to himself.' She stalked across to him and shoved the redundant housekeeper uniform into his hands while Rio dissected that sentence into its relative parts.

'What do you mean, he "can't keep his hands to himself"? Are you saying he touched you?' Astonished by the sudden explosion of anger that was released by that unexpected revelation, Rio was suddenly glad he'd fired Carlos on the spot. His voice cold, he probed for the details. 'Did you report him for sexual harassment?'

'No. I broke his finger.'

'You *broke* his finger?'

'My grandfather taught unarmed combat during the war. He taught me self-defence.'

Distracted by that unexpected confession, Rio looked at her in a new light. 'I'll remember that.'

'You should. But, to repeat, you're not solving *our* problem, Mr Zaccarelli, you're solving *your* problem.'

'Call me Rio. I think we moved on to the first name stage about an hour ago. And, if it weren't for you, we wouldn't have a problem.' His observation appeared to act as fuel to her already happily burning temper.

'If creepy Carlos hadn't used me, then he would have used someone else and frankly I wish he had because then I wouldn't be in this mess.' She paced the room, trying to work off her stress.

Watching all that fabulous hair ripple down her back, Rio fought the urge to flatten her against the nearest hard surface and conduct in-depth research into the impact of extremely long legs on the enhancement of sexual pleasure.

He had no idea what her true role had been in what he now recognised as a final desperate attempt to stop this deal going through. Maybe she *was* innocent. Maybe she wasn't. Either way, she was the means by which he was going to extract himself from the catastrophic mess he now found himself in.

The upside of his plan was that he didn't need to struggle to keep his hands off her. In fact, the more hands the better.

He was slightly puzzled by her lack of confidence. Accustomed to women so narcissistic that they used every reflective surface to admire themselves, it came as a shock to discover one who didn't seem to spend her time in endless self-admiration. When she'd confessed that men found her too tall it had been on the tip of his tongue to point out that height was irrelevant when you were horizontal, but he'd managed not to voice that thought aloud. Rio wondered whether it would count as a charitable act to demonstrate just how well those endless legs of hers would wrap around his waist.

'You look perfect in that dress.'

'I look like a politician or something.' Keeping her back to him, she paced towards the window and Rio frowned.

'Don't go near the windows.' His clipped command earned him a challenging glance.

'Why? We're too high up for anyone to see.'

'In today's world of long lenses?' Watching her lose more colour from her face, he let the observation hang in the air. 'The next photograph they take of us will be when I'm ready and not before.'

'I don't want any more photographs taken!' But she moved away from the window, fiddling nervously with the fabric of her dress as she paced in the other direction. 'Look—this whole engagement thing is ridiculous. Can't you just stop that photo being printed?'

'No.' Rio recoiled from the sheen of tears he saw in her eyes. 'But I can stop it looking like a sleazy one-night stand. We're going to make people believe we're in a relationship—serious about each other.' Looking at her now, those high heels elongating her spectacular legs, he was even starting to believe it could work. No red-blooded male would question his interest.

'It's a really s-stupid plan.'

Rio, who had been congratulating himself on a truly genius idea, was insulted. 'It's an incredible plan.' His tone cooled. 'You're lucky I'm not currently involved with anyone.'

'Lucky?'

Rio dismissed thoughts of the Russian ballerina. 'It's un-usual for me not to be in a relationship.'

'Well, I suppose that's one of the advantages of being filthy rich. Where there's money, there will always be women.'

Taken aback by that diminution of his qualities, Rio breathed deeply. 'Women are generally interested in more than my wallet.'

'How do you know? They're not going to tell you, are

they? And I don't suppose gold-diggers come with a warning hanging round their neck.'

'I can spot a gold-digger in the dark from a thousand paces.' He ignored the discordant image in his head that reminded him that on at least one occasion that statement had proven not to be true.

'Good for you.' Her slightly acidic tone matched her growing agitation. She explored the room, picking things up and putting them down again. First the vase on the table, then a notepad, then a remote control. She squinted down at it and pressed a button mindlessly and a gas fire flared to life behind a glass panel in the wall.

Swearing under his breath, Rio crossed the room and turned her to face him. 'I know you're anxious that they're going to print your photograph but, trust me, it will be fine providing people think we're together. This is the best way of dealing with it.'

'That's just your opinion.'

Rio, who had never before had his opinion dismissed, ground his teeth. 'If you have an alternative suggestion, then I'm listening.'

'No, you're not. You're pretending to listen while secretly thinking that you'll let me say my piece and then just do what you were planning to do all along, but it isn't going to work. I won't pretend to be engaged to you.'

Assuming that her reluctance was rooted in her insecurity, Rio sought to reassure her. 'By the time we've done something about your wardrobe, your nails and your hair, it will be easy to convince people that we are involved with each other.'

'Is that supposed to make me feel better?' She put the remote control down slowly and carefully, as if it were a potential murder weapon. *'You'll look fine, Evie, once I've turned you into something decent. Is that what you're saying?'*

Her tightly worded question triggered all the alarms in Rio's internal warning system.

'If this is going to be one of those, *Does my bottom look big in this?* conversations, then don't go there,' he warned, his tone thickened with frustration. The clock was ticking and her resistance was an obstacle he hadn't anticipated. Not for one moment had it entered his head that she'd be anything other than compliant. 'If you hadn't been lying naked on my bed, I would not have been tempted to kiss you,' Rio exploded with the tension that had been building since the photographer had chosen to elbow his way into his life. 'If you had worn clothes or at least slept under the covers—'

'If you had shown some self-control—'

Rio breathed deeply because that was a charge from which it was almost impossible to defend himself and that particular aspect of this whole seedy situation disturbed him far more than he was prepared to admit. He was always extremely careful with his liaisons and he never indulged in one-night stands. And yet where had his self-control been a few hours ago when he'd seen her lying on his bed? Not for the first time, he wondered what would have happened had the photographer paused before taking his photograph. *How much more revealing and incriminating would a later picture have been?*

'There is no point in dwelling on what is done,' he said tautly, 'and the truth is that a photograph of you naked in that bed was all that was needed. The rest would have been easily created from association and artistic use of Photoshop.'

'You mean they would have manufactured a photograph of the two of us together?'

'Photography software is increasingly sophisticated and you *were* in my bedroom. Stop throwing out obstacles when the solution I'm proposing is in both our interests. Your reputation stays intact. You mentioned that you have nowhere to live—I'm offering you somewhere to live. You get to stay here, in the most highly prized hotel suite in London. Anything you want, you can have. Most women in your position would be extremely excited at the prospect of an all expenses paid holiday complete with shopping.'

'Women are not a homogeneous breed, Mr Zaccarelli— we're individuals with individual tastes and needs. And why do you care so much about whether it looks like a one-night stand or something more? What is this deal you keep talking about?'

The question caught him off guard. For a brief moment he felt his control start to unravel. 'You don't need to know. Rest assured that I have a whole team of lawyers working night and day to make sure that it doesn't fall apart at the eleventh hour.'

'And if it does?'

A chill ran down his spine. 'It won't.'

'Providing I do as you say. I don't understand why this story could ruin it for you. Is this deal of yours with some old-fashioned guy who thinks you should have a blameless reputation or something?'

'Something like that.' Rio realised that his palms were sweating and he turned away from her, locking down his emotions with ruthless efficiency.

'So you'll do all this to win one deal? Money, money, money. Is that all that matters to you?' Increasingly agitated, she rubbed her hands down her arms. 'Well, I'm sorry if my decision loses you a few million, but I'm not prepared to do it.'

Back in control, Rio turned to look at her, sure that he must have misheard. 'Excuse me?'

'I won't do it. I'm just going to look more of a fool.' She covered her face with her hands and gave a moan of embarrassment. 'Every time I think about that photo being printed I just want to hide. Grandpa is never going to be able to hold his head up at senior poker ever again.'

Banking down his own frustration, Rio crossed the room. Gently, he pulled her hands away from her face. 'You are not going to hide. You are going to hold your head up high and look as though you are in love with me.' Appreciating the irony of his own words, he gave a faint smile and she instantly picked up on it.

'Don't tell me—usually you're telling women *not* to fall in love with you.'

'I'm not into serious relationships. They don't work for me. I'm not that kind of guy.' *Once, just once, and look where it had got him.*

'And I assume the public know that.'

'If you're worried that I won't be able to play my part, then don't be. I can be very convincing,' Rio assured her. 'The fact that I'm not usually serious about a woman will make this whole story all the more plausible.'

'And all the more embarrassing.'

Rio's jaw clenched and he spoke through his teeth, his patience severely tested. 'Are you saying it's embarrassing to be associated with me?'

'I'm saying it's going to be embarrassing when it ends. For all your so-called brilliant brain, you haven't thought this through. It's going to end—and then how will it look?'

'What does it matter?' Irritated to the point of explosion, Rio spread his hands in a gesture of exasperation. 'Relationships end all the time—it is a part of life. And that is surely a better option for you than having the world think you had a one night stand.'

'So basically I have two choices here—either I get to look like a big, fat slut or I get to be the only woman to be dumped twice in the space of months. Forgive me if I'm not jumping up and down with excitement at either option.'

'Relationships end. I still don't see the problem.'

Her eyes sparked. 'That's because you're only thinking

about yourself as usual. Not me. Have you ever been dumped, Mr Zaccarelli?'

'Rio.'

'Rio—' Using his name brought a flush to her cheeks. 'Has anyone ever told you they don't want to be with you any more?'

'No, of—' He caught himself and shrugged. 'No.'

'You were going to say *of course not*, weren't you?' She gave a disbelieving laugh. 'You are so monumentally arrogant and sure of yourself, but that explains why you can't understand my problem. You don't know what it's like to be rejected.'

'Given that this isn't a real relationship,' Rio said tightly, 'it wouldn't be a real rejection.'

'But if you're going to be as convincing as you say you are, then everyone is going to think it is! Six weeks ago my fiancé, a man I'd known since I was a child, called off our wedding—' She wrapped her arms around herself as if she were suddenly cold. 'Forgive me if I'm not rushing forward to embrace another public battering of my ego. It was bad enough the first time, having everyone feeling sorry for me. I couldn't even walk down the street without ten people saying they understood how hideously humiliated I must feel—this would be a thousand times worse. Only this time it wouldn't be just the village; it would be the whole world.'

'How would that be worse?' Genuinely baffled, struggling to understand, Rio stared at her. 'Why would you care what a bunch of strangers think?'

'I just would! I don't want loads of people I don't know discussing the fact that you dumped me. "Well, it's hardly surprising, is it?"' she parroted. '"I mean, what would a guy like him see in a girl like her?"'

'You'd rather they thought you'd had a sleazy one-night stand with me?'

She gulped. 'No. I'd rather they weren't talking about me at all. But I especially don't want them speculating on why I always get dumped.'

Aware that the clock was ticking and that they needed to get on with this if it was going to have any chance of working, Rio rubbed his hand over the back of his neck and applied his mind to a solution. 'I'll put out an announcement telling everyone you're a wonderful woman and that I have huge respect for you.'

She cringed. 'That would make people feel even *more* sorry for me.'

'I'll say that we will always be friends.'

'Which is basically like saying our relationship fizzled because you don't find me attractive.'

Trying to conceal his mounting exasperation, Rio inhaled deeply and offered up the only other solution that presented itself. 'If it's the dumping part that really worries you, then *you* can dump *me*.'

She stared at him. 'Sorry?'

'I'll allow you to dump me,' he said tightly. 'Problem solved.'

'That wouldn't work.'

'*Now* what? Why wouldn't it work?'

'Because you're rich and handsome. No one would believe it. Why would anyone in my position dump a man like you?'

'That's easy. I'm a total bastard,' Rio said immediately, relieved to be able to deal with that obstacle so simply. 'No one who knows me will have any trouble believing you kicked me out.' His confession drew a tiny smile from her.

'You're that bad?'

Transfixed by that smile, Rio couldn't look away from her mouth. 'I'm terrible. I'm dominating, I like everything my own way—basically I'm horribly selfish, inwardly focused,

I set myself a punishing schedule and frequently work an eighteen-hour day, which usually means that all I want to do when I'm with a woman is have sex.' *And he wanted to have sex with her, right here, right now.* It exasperated him to realise that, even in this most delicate of situations, he could barely keep his hands off her.

'You manage to fit sex into your punishing working day?' Her voice was faint. 'When?'

'Whenever I feel like it—' He was intrigued by the colour in her cheeks. 'So that's settled then. I'll do something awful—'

'You mean you'll behave the way you usually behave.'

'Something like that.' He acknowledged the barely veiled insult with a dismissive shrug. 'You'll dump me and, just to make sure it looks completely authentic, I'll go round looking moody for a few weeks.'

'So you admit to being selfish, inwardly focused and a total bastard, but no woman has ever dumped you. Why? What have you got going for you?'

Rio gave a slow, confident smile. 'If we're spending the foreseeable future together then you'll have time to discover the answer to that yourself.'

'If you're talking about sex, then you can forget it. Unlike you, I think sex should be part of a relationship.'

'So do I.'

She backed away. 'Yes, but the difference is that you don't want your relationships to go anywhere, and I do. Just so that there's no misunderstanding, I'm telling you now that I'll be sleeping in the second bedroom.'

Rio, who had his own ideas about where she'd be sleeping, decided to handle that issue later. 'So you'll do it? Good. And, when the time comes, you dump me.'

'I still don't see how we can convince them that we're together.'

'By being seen together,' he said smoothly, taking her

hand and hauling her against him. 'The first thing you need is a ring, so let's go. I'm about to buy you the biggest diamond you've ever seen.'

'I've never been in a chauffeur driven car. There's masses of room.' Evie stretched her legs out in front of her, aware that Rio was watching her with amusement.

'That's the general idea.'

'Why do you need so much room? You could have a party in here.'

'Not a party, but sometimes I do conduct business meetings in the car if I'm travelling short distances.'

'What happens for long distances?'

'I use my private jet.'

Evie gave a choked laugh. 'Private jet. Of course. This year's *must have* accessory. No serious tycoon should be seen without one.'

'Not an accessory,' he drawled, 'but a practical, money-saving tool.'

'Money-saving.' Evie nodded, struggling to keep her face straight as she slid her hand over the soft leather seat. 'Of course. I find the same thing. When I'm economizing, I turn down the heating and watch my food budget but I always make sure I leave the private jet well alone. As you say, it's such a practical, money-saving tool.'

'This may surprise you, but when you spend as many hours in the air as I do, that becomes a truth.'

As the gulf in their lifestyles opened up between them, Evie's smile faltered and she flopped back against the seat. 'This is ridiculous,' she muttered. 'It's never going to work. Give me one reason why a guy like you would ever be involved with a woman like me?'

'You have incredible legs.' He moved so quickly that she didn't anticipate it. Before she had time to respond, his hand was buried in her hair and his mouth descended on hers in a kiss that sent her brain spinning. 'I love the way you taste,' he murmured huskily and she gasped against his lips.

'OK, enough, you don't have to keep kissing me—' Seriously unsettled by the way he made her feel, Evie shoved at his chest, alarmed when he didn't budge. She'd always considered herself pretty strong for a woman but her violent push had no effect on him. 'It was kissing me that got us in this mess—'

'But now we're in this "mess", as you call it, we might as well enjoy it. They'll believe it, *tesoro,* once they see you.' He showed no inclination to stop what he was doing. 'You have amazing hair, fantastic breasts—'

Evie moaned as his mouth trailed along her jaw. 'Those are all physical things. That's just sex.'

'Never underestimate the power of sex. Sex is a very important part of a relationship.' One hand slid down her back to her bottom and Evie wriggled away, mortified.

'Don't do that—'

'Why not?'

'Well, for a start because someone might see you—'

His eyes gleamed into hers. 'And that would be a problem because—?'

Evie could hardly breathe. For a moment she'd forgotten that the whole objective of this charade was for people to see them. Confused, she wondered whether he was faking the attraction. But then she remembered the kiss that had started all this…

'Unless people have X-ray vision, they're not going to be able to see your hand on my bottom,' she croaked and he gave a wicked smile as he ran his fingers through her hair.

'Any red-blooded male glancing into this car will have a pretty accurate idea of the location of my missing hand.'

'You're not funny.' She'd barely thought about sex before she'd met him. Now she was finding it hard to think about anything else. Was he going to keep kissing her? Did he think she was made of stone? Embarrassed by the burning heat between her thighs, Evie pulled away from him and this time he released her, smiling slightly as he watched her shift to the furthest corner of her seat.

His whole attitude should have been enough to make her dislike him, but instead she found herself alarmingly turned on by the electric combination of smooth sophistication and command. It was humiliating, she thought, squirming in her seat, to find a man as basic as Rio so attractive. But evidently she wasn't the only one. After all, *he'd* never been dumped...

They were driving through the upmarket streets of Knightsbridge. The windows of Harrods, the world famous store, were decorated for Christmas and everywhere she looked there were rich-looking women wearing fur and dark glasses, stepping out of expensive-looking cars.

By the time Rio's driver pulled up outside an exclusive jewellers, Evie had lost all desire to be seen in public. Even in the smart outfit and sexy shoes, she didn't fit.

Two guards stood either side of the heavy glass door and, even from the protective cocoon of Rio's car, she could see that the few pieces on display in the window would have satisfied royalty.

Thoroughly intimidated, she thought about the tiny diamond that Jeff had given her when he'd proposed. At the time she'd thought it was small because they were saving for a deposit so that they could buy their own cottage. Now she realised it had been small because he'd been spending most of their shared savings on his other girlfriend.

She'd been a total idiot. But it was partly her fault, wasn't it? She and Jeff had grown up together. Everyone had assumed that one day they'd get married. Evie had told herself that the fact she felt no spark was because she wasn't a particularly passionate person. She'd assumed Jeff was the same.

And then she'd discovered what he'd been doing with Cindy, the librarian from the next village...

She stole a sideways glance at Rio, her gaze resting on his mouth, remembering the sizzling, steamy kiss. Sparks had been shooting all over the place.

And now she was expected to pretend they were in a relationship.

'You expect me to go in there? Why can't they come to us? In the movies you just pick up the phone and loads of jewellers come running to the hotel with a selection of rings.'

'In the movies, they're not trying to attract the interest of the paparazzi.' Rio leaned across her to undo her seat belt. 'If I'd ordered them to bring the rings to the hotel, it wouldn't have been anywhere near as loud a statement.'

Flattening herself to the seat, Evie stared at him, determined not to be impressed. 'I still don't understand how this is going to work. If the whole point of this is to get the paparazzi to take a photograph of us, shouldn't someone have called them and told them we're here?'

'No need. Wherever I go, you can find photographers.' Rio's tone was bored. 'It's part of my life, which means it's now part of your life. Get used to it.' As the driver opened the door Rio gestured for her to leave the car but Evie didn't budge.

'You mean there might be someone out there with a camera? Am I supposed to smile and wave?'

'You're not the Queen,' Rio said dryly. 'Just act normally.'

'But none of this is normal for me! I wouldn't find myself in front of rows of paparazzi,' Evie said irritably. 'I don't know what I'd do. Look over my shoulder, probably, to see who they were photographing because it certainly wouldn't be me. Unless they were taking snaps for a Miss Unbelievably Big Bottom contest.'

'If you mention your bottom again, I will be forced to strip you naked and examine it in detail,' Rio promised silkily and Evie exited the car faster than rum from a bottle.

Just as he'd predicted, a flashlight immediately exploded in her face and she would have stopped if he hadn't propelled her forwards through the doors that had been opened for him as soon as he'd stepped out of the car.

'I thought you wanted to be seen,' Evie hissed under her breath and he curved his hand around her waist and guided her into the exclusive store.

'I never talk to the press,' he purred. 'I never give interviews. I have no intention of altering that pattern. We want this to look as authentic as possible, remember?'

Exasperated, Evie stared up at him. 'How are they supposed to know we're engaged if you don't tell them?' Her face cleared. 'Oh—I get it. I'm supposed to strategically flash the ring on the way out.'

'We'll leave by the back entrance so that no one will see us. In the event that there is a photographer covering the rear of the building, you hide the ring. You put your left hand in your pocket so that no one can get the shot.'

'So we're buying a ring to convince them we're engaged, but we're not going to let them see it?'

'That's right.'

'Have you banged your head or something? You're not making sense.'

'I'm making perfect sense.'

'Not to me. If we go out of the back of the building it's going to look as though we don't want them to see us.'

'Exactly right.' He smiled at the manager who was hovering discreetly. 'Franco—'

'Signor Zaccarelli—' the man oozed deference '—it's good to see you again.'

'Again? How many women have you brought here?' Evie muttered under her breath, but the only indication that Rio had heard her was his vice-like grip on her hand. 'Squeeze any tighter and you'll break my fingers and then you won't get a ring over my knuckle.'

Rio released his grip and urged her forward. 'We need a diamond, Franco.' He glanced down at Evie, a smile on his lips. 'A very special diamond for a very special woman.'

Evie was about to tell him that his smooth talk wasn't the slightest bit convincing when he lowered his mouth and kissed her.

Somewhere in the distance, through the swirling clouds of desire that descended on her brain, she heard one of the sales assistants sigh with envy.

To her, it appeared completely staged but apparently Franco was convinced because he smiled, almost convulsing with delight as he led them through to a private room. 'A very special diamond. Of course. You've come to the right place.'

Evie sat there shell-shocked from the invasive pressure of his mouth, wishing they'd had a conversation about how they were going to play this. Had he said anything about kissing? And what was she supposed to do about the ring? Was she supposed to pick the least expensive one? Or maybe that didn't matter. Presumably a man who considered a private jet to be an 'economy' wouldn't care about the price of a diamond. Or maybe he was planning to ask for a refund when this was over.

She threw Rio an agonized look but he simply smiled. The fact that he was so relaxed simply added to her growing tension.

More aware than ever of the differences between them, Evie shifted uncomfortably and was about to say something when a slender girl entered the room carrying a box.

A hush fell over the room and Evie glanced around her, wondering what was going on. Why was everyone silent?

'It's the Apoletta diamond,' Franco told them in reverent

tones, taking the box from the girl and opening it himself. 'A thing of beauty and perfection, like your love.'

Evie was about to suggest that if the ring was supposed to be a manifestation of their relationship then a small lump of coal might be more appropriate, but one look at Rio's face stopped her. He was looking at her with such intensity that for a moment she stopped breathing and, during that one intimate glance, she made the unsettling discovery that she was as vulnerable to his particular brand of sexual magnetism as all the other women in the room. Even armed with his frank admission of his long list of deficiencies, she couldn't control the explosion of excitement that held her in its grip.

Rio ignored a question from Franco, his attention entirely on her. Then he slid his hand behind her neck and slowly but deliberately kissed her mouth, his lips lingering against hers for long enough to send her heart racing frantically out of control.

'Ti amo,' he said huskily and Evie, dazed by the look as much as the kiss, wondered what it would feel like if a man looked at you like that and meant it.

Without taking his eyes from hers, Rio removed the ring from its velvet nest and slid it onto her finger with cool, confident hands and an unmistakable sense of purpose.

Evie stared down at the incredible diamond, thinking about the sunny morning a few months earlier when Jeff had done the same thing. The ring Jeff had given her had been too big for her finger, whereas this one—'It's exactly the right size.'

'Like Cinderella,' one of the girls sighed and Evie frowned, wondering what was meant by that remark. Did she look as though she'd been cleaning the cellar in rags?

'She means that it's a perfect fit,' Rio said dryly, apparently developing a sudden ability to read her mind. 'And she's right. It's a perfect fit. We won't have to have it adjusted.'

Finding the fact that it fitted slightly spooky, Evie wondered whether it was a fluke or whether Rio was as skilled at guessing the size of her finger as he was her underwear and dress size.

Good guesswork or a man experienced with women?

Another girl entered the room. 'I just thought you should know that it's a media circus out the front.' She sounded apologetic. 'I have no idea how they discovered you were here. Someone must have tipped them off.'

Rio's jaw tightened and for a moment Evie genuinely believed he was annoyed.

'Do you have another entrance?'

'Yes, sir.'

He made a swift phone call and rose to his feet, drawing Evie close to him. 'My driver will meet us out the back. That way, no one should see us.'

Evie hurried alongside him, conscious of the strength of his fingers locked with hers as they were led towards the back of the store. 'Rio—' she hissed his name '—don't we have to pay or something? I don't want to set the alarms off and have to spend Christmas in custody, if it's all the same to you.'

He didn't slacken his stride. 'It's been dealt with.'

'How? Where?'

But he simply propelled her to the back of the store. Moments later, Rio's driver was speeding through the back streets of London's most exclusive area.

Evie flopped back against the seat, twisting the ring on her finger. She tilted her hand, admiring it from every angle, watching as it sparkled and glinted. 'I still don't understand why you went to all that trouble to buy a ring if you're not going to let anyone see it. You didn't even let them see you leave the shop.'

'They know I've left. The fact that I'm being secretive will make them more interested.'

'I hope you don't have an over-inflated idea of your own

importance. Otherwise, this whole idea is going to fall flat on its face.'

Rio's response to that was to hold out his phone. 'Call your grandfather.'

'What, now?' Evie had been putting off that moment and her stomach plummeted as she anticipated what her severe, principled grandfather would say about her current situation. 'What am I supposed to say? Hi, Grandpa, you may be seeing a picture of me naked in today's papers so I just wanted to tell you that I'm not starting a career as a glamour model—'

'It won't be in today's papers. It's too late for that. There's a strong chance it will make tomorrow's editions, but it may already be up on the Internet. Call.'

'My grandfather doesn't surf the Internet. He's eighty-six,' Evie squeaked but her observation merely earned her a lift of an eyebrow.

'What does his age have to do with anything?'

'You wouldn't be asking me that if you'd been to the Cedar Court Retirement Home. They celebrated when they got a decent TV picture. They probably think high speed broadband is another type of dressing for varicose veins.'

He didn't withdraw the phone. 'Call.'

'I can't.' Evie's voice was a whisper and she shrank back against the seat as she tried to delay the inevitable. 'This is the guy who took me on my first day at school. He taught me to ride a bike. He doesn't believe in holding hands or kissing in public. I'm all he has in the world and he thinks I'm a really decent, old-fashioned girl… In fact, I *am* a decent, old fashioned girl, or I was until I met you.'

'All the more reason to call him before he hears it from someone else.'

Running out of excuses, Evie took the phone reluctantly. Her hand shook as she keyed in the number. As she waited for him to answer, she pressed her fingers to the bridge of her nose and tried not to think about how disappointed her grandfather was going to be.

After all he'd done for her, after all his love and affection, he didn't deserve this...

'Grandpa? It's Evie...how are you doing?' Her voice sounded false to her and she wondered how long it would take her grandfather to pick up on the fact that something was wrong. 'Are you staying warm there in all this snow?' Maybe that was a good link, she thought desperately as she listened to his cheerful response—*I was a bit too warm, Grandpa, so I thought I'd take my clothes off...*

'No, nothing's wrong; I just thought I'd ring you for a chat.' Aware that Rio was watching her, Evie carried on making small talk about the weather and listening to her grandfather's observations about his friends. When he mentioned that he'd been boasting about her again to Mrs Fitzwilliam, two huge tears slipped from Evie's eyes and she covered her mouth with her hand.

With a sigh, Rio removed the phone from her. 'Mr Anderson? Rio Zaccarelli here—no, we haven't met, but I know your granddaughter—yes, I'm the same Zaccarelli that owns the hotel and spa chain—' he leaned back in his seat, not looking remotely discomfited by the prospect of dealing with what could only be described as a hideously awkward situation '—yes, it's still doing well, despite the economic climate—absolutely—' he smiled '—that's how I met Evie—'

Worried that Rio might actually say something that would make things even worse, Evie gulped down her tears and tried to grab the phone but he held it out of reach, laughing at something her grandfather had just said.

'I've already learned that to my cost—yes, she is—'

Evie frowned. 'I am what? What are you saying?'

Rio ignored her. 'I know about that. Yes, she told me. But his loss is my gain.'

Were they talking about her broken engagement? Evie covered her eyes with her hands, all too able to imagine what her grandfather was saying.

'Yes, a total loser—' Rio's voice became several shades cooler '—she's better off without him... No, not too badly—that's what we rang to tell you. We're engaged. I know it seems sudden but you can blame me for that—when I see something I want, I have to have it and I've never felt like this about a woman before.'

Evie peeped through her fingers and waited for Rio to pass the phone across so that she could receive a giant telling off from her strict grandfather. Instead, she heard laughter as Rio controlled the conversation.

'We wanted to warn you that there might be some revealing photographs in the press. My fault entirely—they follow me around, I'm afraid—' Rio's voice was smooth and he gave a slight smile in response to something her grandfather said. 'I agree—I've always said the same thing—that's right. No—no, she's fine—just a bit embarrassed because she's pretty shy about that sort of stuff... Yes, I know she's modest—' he shot her an ironic glance '—well, I have my lawyers onto it but if anyone mentions it to you, you can tell them the photographer was trespassing in a private room—yes, I'll hand you over—good to talk to you—look forward to meeting you in person—' Having moulded her rock-hard war veteran grandfather into the consistency of porridge, Rio handed her the phone, a smug expression on his face. 'He's delighted. He wants to congratulate you in person.'

Evie tentatively lifted the phone to her ear. 'Grandpa—?' She was unable to get a word in edgeways as her grandfather told her how delighted he was that she'd finally met a real man and proceeded to spend the next five minutes extolling Rio's virtues, all of which appeared to centre around his ability to buck the market and grow his business, no matter what the economic challenges. The issue of the naked photograph appeared to have been absorbed along with all the other news.

Finally, her grandfather drew breath. 'Answer me one question—are you in love with him, Evie? That's all I want to know.'

Oh, dear God, how was she supposed to answer that? 'I—'

'It doesn't matter that a man is rich—what matters is whether there's strength and responsibility in his character. Rio Zaccarelli has all those qualities, but none of it matters if you don't love him.'

Talk about out of the frying pan into the fire. In order to stop her grandfather thinking she'd had a one-night stand, she'd gone along with Rio's idea but suddenly she was being sucked deeper and deeper into the charade.

Knowing her grandfather would worry, she gave the only answer she could. 'I love him, Grandpa.' She scowled as Rio raised his eyebrows, amusement shimmering in his black eyes. Doubtless he was so used to hearing besotted women say those words that he barely registered them.

Her grandfather sounded ecstatic. 'So it looks as though I might be bouncing that great-grandchild on my knee next Christmas after all.'

Great-grandchild?

Evie's mouth dropped in dismay. Somehow she'd gone from naked in bed, to engaged and then straight to pregnant!

How was she ever going to unravel this mess?

Hoping Rio hadn't overheard that particular part of the conversation, she lowered her head, allowing her hair to fall forward in a curtain, shielding her face. 'Well—let's just see how things go, Grandpa—no hurry—'

'Of course there's a hurry! I'm not getting any younger—'

'Don't say that. You know I hate it.' The thought of losing him horrified her and, when Evie finally ended the call, her hands were still shaking. Listening to her grandfather's animated voice had made her feel hideously guilty.

Oblivious to her mounting distress, Rio took the phone from her, smiling with satisfaction. 'That went well.'

She rounded on him, her eyes glistening with tears. '*That did not go well, Rio!* I just lied to my eighty-six-year-old grandfather. How do you think that makes me feel?'

'A great deal better than having to tell your eighty-six-year-old grandfather why you had a one-night stand with a man you'd never met before,' he said coldly. 'Calm down. If there happen to be any paparazzi around, I'd rather they didn't print the fact that we were having a row within ten minutes of putting the rock on your finger. Your grandfather was delighted to hear that we're together—a little surprised, perhaps, but basically pleased. I'm considered an incredible catch. You don't have anything to worry about.'

He reminded her of an armoured tank, forging forwards regardless of what was in his path. Her feelings were no more than blades of grass, easily squashed and ignored under the weight of his own driving sense of purpose.

When Rio Zaccarelli wanted something, he got it. And apparently he was willing to go to any lengths to secure this particular 'deal'.

'Why didn't I think this through? I've just raised his hopes and that's an awful thing to do.' Frantic, Evie reached for the phone again. 'I have to tell him the truth, now, before this whole thing escalates and he tells everyone I'm marrying a billionaire.'

'Leave it.'

'Rio, he thinks I'm going to get pregnant any moment! He wants to bounce his great-grandchild on his knee! I'm sorry, but I can't do this.'

But Rio had slipped the phone back into the inside pocket of his jacket. 'You agreed to the plan.'

'Because you railroaded me. I didn't have time to think it

through, but I can see now this is going to be really complicated and—'

'It's done. Too late.' With an infuriating lack of emotion,
he scanned the screen of his BlackBerry. 'The switchboard
at my corporate headquarters is jammed with journalists
seeking confirmation that I've just become engaged. The
story is out there.'

Her stomach lurched. 'And your people have confirmed
it?'

'They've said "no comment", which is as good as demanding that the press print an announcement. It's too late
to change your mind now. Stop panicking. Your grandfather
sounded fine about the whole thing. Tell me about Jeff.'

Evie tried to ignore the throbbing pain behind her eyes. 'I
don't want to talk about Jeff.'

'I'm not surprised.' Rio sprawled in his seat, texting with
astonishing speed and dexterity. 'He sounds like a total
loser.'

Evie stared at him in helpless disbelief. She wanted to
explain how worried she was about hurting her grandfather's
feelings, but she knew she was wasting her time. Rio Zaccarelli
didn't care about feelings, did he? All he cared about was
making sure his business proceeded unhindered.

'I really don't think I can go through with this.'

Rio watched her, a deadly gleam in his eyes. 'We made a
deal.'

'Yes.' Evie croaked the word, knowing that she was
trapped. If this was the only way to prevent that photograph
being published, then she had no choice.

Deals, deals, deals…

She'd made a deal with the devil. And now she was going
to pay.

CHAPTER FIVE

DRAGGING her aching limbs into the Penthouse suite, Evie toed off her shoes in relief and crumpled onto the rug. 'How does anyone walk in these things?' Staring up at the ceiling, she moved her toes gingerly. 'I feel as though both my legs have been chewed by a shark.'

'That is why you are lying on the floor?' Rio paused in mid-text, his eyes bright with incredulity. 'If you're tired, lie on the sofa.'

'I can't make it that far. I may never walk again.' Evie gave a long groan and flexed her sore feet. 'I bet you've never tried to squash your feet into a torture device before. Who invented heels? The Spanish Inquisition?'

Rio pocketed his phone, scooped her up and deposited her on the sofa.

'Oh—that's better.' Evie rolled on her side and closed her eyes, trying not to think about how his hands had felt on her skin. *How strong he was.*

'Most women find shopping a pleasurable pastime.'

'Yes, well, most women don't have to buy an entire wardrobe after just three hours sleep, and most women aren't shopping with *you*.' Yawning, Evie snuggled into the soft pile of cushions, twisting and turning to find a comfortable position. 'You said "no" so many times I thought that poor stylist person was going to throw herself out of the window.

I thought the objective was to have a high visibility shopping trip, not give some innocent woman a nervous breakdown.'

'I was trying to achieve a compromise between "wholesome" and "sexy", which proved to be something of a challenge.'

'Why do I have to look sexy?'

'Because it's important that you look like someone I'd date.'

Squashed flat by that comment, Evie curled up in a ball. 'Do you have any idea how insulting you are? Once in a while you could think about my feelings, otherwise I'm going to dump you long before this farce is supposed to end. And it doesn't really matter what the clothes look like, does it? It isn't as if we're going anywhere.' She glanced round the Penthouse, taking in the luxury. Something seemed different about the place, but she couldn't work out what. 'You won't even let me look out of the window in case someone takes my picture.'

'Astonishingly enough, I *am* thinking of you. It's precisely because we are going out that I expended all that time and effort in making sure you had an appropriate wardrobe,' he gritted. 'Tonight you're going to be walking down that red carpet with film stars and celebrities—I didn't want you to feel out of place.'

'Red carpet? What red carpet?' Evie shot upright. 'You didn't say anything about going out. I thought we were in hiding.'

'We were creating gossip and speculation which, by tonight, will have spread sufficiently to ensure that if that photograph appears it will be taken as confirmation that we are seriously involved.' Rio walked over to the desk and switched on his laptop. 'We have to be seen out together which, unfortunately, means that tonight we have to attend a film premiere and a charity ball.'

'Unfortunately? It's unfortunate that we have to attend a

film premiere and a charity ball?' Assuming he was joking, Evie started to laugh and then she saw the tension in his shoulders and the grim expression on his handsome face and realised that he was serious. He didn't want to go.

Her sudden excitement evaporated and she deflated like a balloon at a children's party. Her brain scanned all the possible reasons for his dark, forbidding scowl. 'You don't want to be seen with me.'

'*Obviously* I do,' he said tightly, 'given that it is the entire purpose of going.'

Evie sat with her back stiff, picking at her fingernails, telling herself that it was ridiculous to feel hurt by that comment. 'I understand that you feel you have to do it. But the reason you don't want to go is because you're embarrassed to be seen out with me.'

'I don't want to go because I'm incredibly busy at the moment.'

Something about the way he held himself told her that he was lying. Whatever was wrong, it had nothing to do with his workload. 'But we're going anyway?'

'Yes. We'll show our faces and then leave.' With a single tap of his finger, he brought a spreadsheet up on the screen. 'Wear the silver dress.'

Shimmering silver, Evie thought absently. *With swept-up hair.*

She should have felt thrilled but instead she felt the most crushing disappointment. 'What's the point of making a fuss if we're only going to stay five minutes?' The fact that he wasn't even looking at her increased her anger. 'It's hardly worth getting dressed, is it?'

'A brief visit is perfectly normal at these things. There is no point in wasting a whole evening when our purpose can be achieved in a short space of time.'

There was a tension in the room that she didn't understand. 'What if your purpose is to enjoy yourself?'

He was frowning at the screen. 'We're talking about a throng of people, none of whom have the slightest interest in anyone but themselves and their own self-advancement. As it happens, I have a very specific reason for going to this particular ball—I need to speak to Vladimir Yartsev.'

'Who is he?'

'Don't you read newspapers?'

Evie flushed. 'Sometimes. When I'm not working.'

'Vladimir Yartsev is a Russian oil oligarch. A very powerful man.'

'But not as powerful as you.'

A ghost of a smile touched his mouth. 'Different power.'

Evie curled her legs underneath her. 'Alternative energy. Like fossil fuels versus a wind farm.' Looking at the thin line of his mouth, she sighed. 'Sorry. I forgot you don't have a sense of humour. So this guy is going to be sitting at our table? I presume you want me to be extra-nice to him?'

'That won't be possible. He doesn't speak much English and I doubt his interpreter will be there.' Rio altered one of the figures on the spreadsheet. 'I'm sure if you smile at him it won't do any harm.'

His comment was so derogatory that she almost thumped him.

He made assumptions about people. Evie watched him, knowing that she was going to have the last laugh on this particular point. 'I won't need an interpreter. I'm good at communicating with people.' She was purposely vague. 'So you're hoping to meet up with this Vladimir guy—who else? Doesn't anyone just go to have fun?'

'They go to be seen. And at a charity ball they go to be seen spending money. It's a game. I go because there are a few contacts I need to make. I have no doubt it will be boring.'

'Thanks. So basically you're saying that not only do I

not look right, but I bore you. I can see we're in for a great evening.'

'I was talking about the other guests—' his tone was thickened with exasperation '—but carry on like this and I'll add you to the list. I've already told you—the reason I don't stay long is because I can't afford the time. I have work to do.'

All he did was work.

But he was taking her to a charity ball and a film premiere.

Evie felt a renewed flutter of excitement at the prospect of playing Cinderella for a night. 'So we're showing our faces at two events—but you have invites to loads more than that?'

'I have seven invitations for this evening. I've picked the two most high profile.' Showing no interest whatsoever in that fact, Rio focused on the screen. 'Normally, a hostess would do her utmost to avoid a clash, but this is Christmas so it's inevitable.'

Christmas.

Suddenly Evie realised what was different about the room. 'Someone's taken down all my decorations.' Horrified, she sprang to her feet and glanced around her. 'The tree has gone. And the holly—why would they have done that?'

'Because I gave instructions that all the decorations should be removed.'

Already bruised from his previous comments, it was hard to keep her voice steady. 'You didn't like the decorations?'

'No.'

She felt numb. 'I took *ages* getting them exactly right. I thought you'd be pleased—'

'I wasn't pleased.'

So she looked wrong, she was boring, and now he was saying she was useless at her job. It was the final straw.

Rio glanced up. 'While I'm staying here, I don't want to know it's Christmas.' His eyes were molten black and menacing. 'I don't want to see a single decoration. Is that clear?'

'Yes. It's perfectly clear.' Her voice high-pitched; deeply offended that he'd criticised her work, Evie stalked into the bedroom, yanking the doors closed behind her.

Her confidence in shreds, she leaned back against the doors.

Miserable, horrible, vile man.

Chemistry? Yes, there was chemistry—but she wished it was the sort that would result in some sort of explosive reaction that would blast him out of her life. He made her feel *small*. He made her feel useless and insignificant. Apparently she couldn't even decorate a Christmas tree to his satisfaction.

She stood for a moment, breathing deeply, horribly hurt by his dismissive comments. In a few sentences he'd shredded her fragile self-confidence.

With a sniff, she tried to tell herself that it didn't matter. Why should she care what he thought? So he hated her decorations. So what? The man was a cold hearted workaholic.

Fancy going to all this trouble just so that he didn't lose out on a stupid business deal.

He made Scrooge look like a cheerleader.

What sort of man would rather work than enjoy a night at a glittering Christmas ball? Did he think his entire business was going to fall apart or something?

Trying not to be hurt by the fact that he clearly wanted to spend as little time as possible in her company, Evie wrenched off the jacket that went with her 'wholesome' dress and flung it over the nearest chair.

Feeling miserable and unappreciated, she undressed and slipped under the covers, wanting to blot out her unhappiness with a much needed afternoon nap. As she closed her eyes she reminded herself that she was doing this so that her grandfather wouldn't be hurt and embarrassed. No other reason.

Once all the fuss had died down, she'd give Rio Zaccarelli the boot. Or should that be 'the stiletto'?

Either way, she was seriously looking forward to *that* day.

Rio fastened the sleeves of his dress shirt. Normally he relished the challenge of a difficult situation. On this occasion the stakes were too high to make the whole issue anything other than stressful. Adding an evening of Christmas celebrations into that mix simply increased the stress.

Get it over with.

There was no sound of activity from the bedroom and Rio wondered whether he should have checked on Evie. She'd been in there all day and they were supposed to be leaving in fifteen minutes. Was she still asleep?

Or was she still sulking over the Christmas decorations?

He was just walking towards the bedroom doors when they opened suddenly.

'Don't say a word. Not a word.' A dangerous glint in her blue eyes, she stalked barefoot across the carpet. A pair of silver shoes dangled from her fingers. 'Every time you open your mouth you say something nasty so, unless red eyes are the latest "must have" accessory on the celebrity circuit, then it's safer if you say nothing.'

Rio was pleased she'd instructed him to say nothing because, for once, the power of speech appeared to have deserted him. He'd been present when she'd tried on the dress—he'd approved it—but clearly he hadn't devoted his full attention to the task because he had no memory of it looking quite this good. Or maybe it was because he'd seen the dress in daylight and it was definitely designed to dazzle at night.

The fabric sparkled with every turn of her body and the effect was incredible—it was as if she were illuminated, each sensuous curve lit up and accentuated by the shimmering fabric. Her hair she'd scooped up and secured to the back of her head with silver clips, the slightly haphazard style both kooky and sexy.

'You look incredible.'

'Wholesome?'

He ignored the sarcasm in her tone. 'Sexy and wholesome. It's an intriguing combination. It would look even more effective if you could stop glaring at me.'

'I'll stop glaring at you when we're in public.' She was as prickly as a porcupine. 'Our deal doesn't include having to like each other, does it?'

Rio clenched his jaw. 'If I offended you, then I apologise.'

'*If?* There is no *if*, Rio. Of course you offended me! You criticised my work and then you criticised me. You're trying to turn me into a clone of the type of woman you date and then you get irritated when I'm not doing things right.'

'That isn't true, but—'

'No!' She lifted her hand like a policeman stopping traffic. 'Don't say anything else. You're incapable of speaking without being offensive.'

Unaccustomed to having to work so hard with a woman, Rio drew in a long, slow breath. 'It's snowing outside and that dress has no back to it. You'll need something to keep you warm—' He handed her a large flat box and she looked at him suspiciously before taking it with a frown.

'Now what? A cloak with a hood so that you can cover my face? A—oh—' she gasped, and then her face lost its colour and she dropped the box containing the snowy-white fur onto the carpet. 'I can't wear that. I won't wear fur.'

'It isn't real.' Wondering whether every interaction was going to result in confrontation, Rio stooped and retrieved it. 'It's fake.'

Evie stood with her hands behind her back. 'You're sure?'

'Positive.' He draped it around her shoulders. Her skin was warm and smooth against the backs of his fingers and he felt the immediate flash of chemistry. Her breathing was shallow and fast and for a moment she stood rigid, a faint bloom of colour lifting the pallor of her cheeks.

'Is that what you do when you offend someone? You buy them an extravagant gift rather than say sorry? Does it work?'

'You tell me. Your hair looks amazing against the white fur.' He saw the pulse beating in her throat and knew that she was feeling exactly what he was feeling.

'Don't think that just because I'm wearing this, I've forgiven you. I can't be bought.'

A woman who couldn't be bought.

Rio gave a faint smile at that concept.

'It does feel *gorgeous* against bare skin.' She wriggled her shoulders in an unconsciously seductive movement that sent his libido into overdrive.

Incredibly aroused, he drew her against him. 'You could remove the dress,' he suggested silkily, 'and just wear the fur.' Even without touching his fingers to her wrist, he knew her pulse was racing and Rio saw something in her eyes seconds before she looked away. *Desire.* Programmed to identify that look, he was about to suggest that the fur would be comfortable to lie on, when she shoved at his chest.

'You just can't help yourself, can you? We're supposed to be stopping the photo looking sleazy and all you want to do is stay in and make the whole situation even tackier. Or is this deal suddenly not important to you?'

Rio froze, horrified by the realisation that for a few precious seconds his mind had been wiped of every thought except for one and that was the erotic possibilities of fur against Evie's pale skin. 'You're right. Let's go.' Seriously disconcerted by the fact that she was so together while he was locked in the savage grip of rampaging hormones, he faced the lowering fact that, had she not stopped him, he would have tumbled her onto the rug in front of the fire and followed his instincts with no thought for anything except the demands of his own super-sized libido.

Exasperated with himself and seriously unsettled, Rio snagged his jacket from the back of the chair and urged her towards the elevator. 'The premiere starts in about fifteen minutes.'

'Great. So we'll be last.'

'That was the intention.' He pressed the button for the ground floor. 'We show ourselves in public when the crowd is at its maximum.'

'Why not? If I'm going to humiliate myself, it might as well be in a big way.'

Evie walked gingerly up the red carpet, relieved that the silver shoes were so much more comfortable than the red ones, her fingers gripping tightly to Rio's rock-hard biceps. Despite the falling snow, there was a huge crowd waiting in the hope of seeing the stars and Evie felt like a fraud as she heard the cheering.

'They're going to feel short-changed when they see me. What am I supposed to do?' She hissed the words between her teeth, her smile never faltering as what felt like a million camera lenses were pointed in her direction. 'Do I flash the ring? Do I look at you adoringly?'

'Just act normally.'

Evie felt a rush of exasperation that he had so little idea how she felt. 'I don't normally walk along red carpets in high heels pretending to be engaged to a very rich man I barely know. Some help here would be appreciated.'

'I'm by your side. That's all the help you need.' He paused to talk to a couple who seemed vaguely familiar. Relieved to see at least two friendly faces and trying to work out where she knew them from, Evie smiled and chatted, finding them surprisingly approachable. She *definitely* knew them from somewhere.

As Rio led her away into the foyer, she was still smiling. 'They were nice. I know I've met them before somewhere—I can't think where—I don't know that many people in London. Do they work at the hotel? What are their names?'

When he told her, she stared at him in mortified silence. 'Right. Both of them Hollywood stars. The reason I know their faces is because I've seen them both in the movies. *Now* I'm embarrassed. Oh, my God—they must have wondered why I was grinning at them like an idiot.'

'You were charming and not at all star-struck. And you didn't ask for their autograph, which is always refreshing.'

'That's because I didn't actually recognise them.' Evie tightened her grip on his arm. 'Do you think they realised? What if I offended them?'

'They enjoyed talking to you and the fact that you were so natural with them suggests that our relationship is an already accepted fact in some circles. You did well. There's no need to make holes in my arm.'

Evie slackened her grip. Determined not to make the same mistake again, she spent the next ten minutes glancing furtively around her, trying to put faces to names. The foyer was crammed with glamorous people, all of whom seemed completely comfortable in their equally glamorous surroundings. They looked like elegant swans, she thought gloomily, whereas she—she felt like an emu. Tall, conspicuous and horribly out of place amongst so many delicate, beautiful birds.

Watching her face, Rio sighed. 'You look as though you're about to visit the dentist. Try and relax.'

Finding the mingling in the foyer desperately stressful, Evie was relieved when they moved into the cinema for the showing of the film. Her spirits lifted still further when she discovered that it was a Christmas movie.

More comfortable in the dark, she slipped off her shoes and settled down in her seat, looking forward to a couple of hours of seasonal entertainment. Watching elves dance across the screen, she was just starting to feel Christmassy when she became aware that Rio was emailing someone on his BlackBerry.

'You're supposed to switch off your mobile.' The moment she said the words she realised how stupid she sounded. This wasn't a commercial showing. It hadn't escaped her notice that the other guests had been vying with each other in an attempt to exchange a few words with him. It was obvious that he was the most powerful, influential guest here. Who was going to tell him off?

Trying to block out the distracting sight of him ploughing through endless emails, Evie turned her attention back to the screen and soon she was lost in the film, sighing wistfully as Santa started putting presents in his sack. 'This is a lovely story,' she said dreamily, 'you really ought to watch it. It might help put you in the Christmas mood.'

The change in him was instantaneous.

Sliding his BlackBerry into the pocket of his dinner jacket, Rio rose to his feet in a purposeful movement, indifferent to the people around him trying to enjoy the film. 'Put your shoes back on. We're going.' Barely giving her time to slide her toes back into the silver shoes, Rio grabbed her hand and led her out of a door at the rear of the cinema.

'They're all looking at us—this is so embarrassing.' Breathless, Evie tried to keep up without twisting her ankle. 'Why are we leaving? I was enjoying myself.'

'I wasn't.' Talking into his phone again, he pushed open a fire door and Evie saw his limousine parked right outside.

'But I only watched about twenty minutes!'

'And that was twenty minutes too long. I can't stand sappy Christmas movies.'

'It hadn't even got going. Santa was about to be set upon by the bad guys determined to ruin Christmas,' Evie gasped, bending her head as he bundled her inside the car. 'Thanks to you, I won't ever find out how it ended.'

'How do you think it ended?' His handsome face was a mask of frustration and tension. 'Happily, of course. It's a Christmas movie. They only ever end happily.'

'I know it ended happily but I wanted to know *how* it ended happily. There's more than one route to a happy ending, you know. It's *how* they do the happy ending that makes it worth watching.'

He shot her a look of exasperation before turning his attention back to the screen of his BlackBerry. 'I would have thought you were too old to believe in happy endings—' he scanned, deleted, emailed '—especially after your recent experience.'

'Just because you haven't encountered a happy ending personally doesn't mean you stop believing in them.'

'If you go through life waiting for a happy ending then you're setting yourself up for permanent disappointment. If you're really that deluded then it's no wonder that you're currently single. No man could hope to live up to your ridiculously high levels of idealism. I almost feel sorry for Jeff.'

Digesting that cynical take on her approach to life, Evie stiffened. 'I gather you don't believe in happy endings. Just don't tell me that you don't believe in Santa or you'll completely ruin my evening.' Intercepting his incredulous glance, she gave him a mocking smile. 'You don't believe in Santa? Careful. If you don't believe, he won't come.'

Shaking his head in despair, Rio turned his head to look out of the window. 'How do you survive in the real world? I thought women like you were extinct.'

'There are some of us still flourishing in the wild.' Evie

leaned her head against the seat and closed her eyes. 'But we're an endangered species. We have to keep our distance from cynics like you who appear to have lost all hope, otherwise we become contaminated.'

'What are you hoping for?'

She kept her eyes firmly shut. There was no way he'd understand and he'd just laugh at her. 'Oh, this and that—the usual sort of stuff.'

'The usual sort of stuff being love, kids and marriage.'

'Go on—laugh. Just because I have my priorities right and all you think about is deals.'

'Trust me—there is *nothing* about love, marriage or kids that makes me want to laugh.'

'And half the world feels the same way as you.' Evie opened her eyes and turned her head to look at him. 'But I don't.'

'Why not? You were dumped six weeks ago.'

'I know.'

'You should be bitter and cynical.'

'How does that help?'

'It stops you having unrealistic expectations.'

'Or perhaps it stops you spotting love when you find it.' Evie adjusted her dress to stop it creasing. 'My grandparents were together for sixty years. I refuse to believe it isn't possible. Finding someone you can love and who loves you back might be rare, but it's not impossible.'

Rio's handsome face was devoid of expression.

Staring into his dark eyes, Evie felt the heat build in her body. 'It's probably different for you,' she said lamely. 'You're rich. Relationships must be even more complicated when you're incredibly wealthy.'

'You've already given me your opinion on the influence of wealth on personal relationships. Clearly you think no woman would entertain the idea of a relationship with me if I weren't wealthy.'

'I didn't say that. I'm sure there are women out there who like cynical men.' She told herself firmly that she wasn't one of them but, even as she gave herself a lecture, she was noticing the blue-black shadow of his hard jaw and the undeniably sexy curve of his mouth. Struggling hard not to think about sex, kissing or anything that required physical contact, Evie tried to lighten the atmosphere. 'If you haven't written your letter to Santa, how do you expect him to know what you'd like?'

'Are you intentionally winding me up?'

'Yes. Is it working?'

'Yes.' A glimmer of a smile pulled at the corners of his mouth and Evie's limbs weakened because he was even more gorgeous when he smiled and because she knew exactly what he could do with that mouth. And she couldn't stop thinking about it. She squirmed with awareness, furious with herself for being such a pushover. Rich, powerful guy—adoring girl. It was an embarrassing cliché.

As if—

'If I'm going along with this plan of yours,' she said quickly, 'there is one other thing I want at the end of it.'

'You can't renegotiate terms once they're agreed,' he said silkily, but Evie lifted her chin, refusing to let him intimidate her.

'I want a job when this is over. And, to be honest, that will look better for you, too. If I'm going to dump you and people find out I've lost my job they'll just assume you're petty and small-minded and you wouldn't want that.'

'Thanks for protecting my image.' His eyes gleamed with sardonic mockery. 'Do you have a particular job in mind? Santa's cheerleader?'

'I was employed to work on Reception,' Evie said firmly, 'and that's what I want to do. I was good at it.'

'So, if you were employed to work on Reception, why were

you working as a housekeeper when I arrived in the early hours this morning?'

'Because Tina demoted me. She said I talked too much.' Evie's eyes flashed defensively. 'But I don't see how you can talk too much as a receptionist. I was making people feel welcome. That's the job my grandfather thinks I'm doing, and that's the job I want when I finally dump you.'

'All right.'

Evie gulped. 'All right? You're saying yes? I can have my job as receptionist back?'

'I'm saying yes,' he drawled softly, 'although, if you're missing your grandfather that much, it strikes me you might be better taking a job closer to home.'

'There isn't anything. I tried that. No one needs my skills. What will happen to Carlos?'

'I have no idea.' Rio pressed a button by his seat and a panel opened. 'Do you drink champagne?'

Evie didn't want to admit she'd never tasted it. 'Of course.'

He withdrew a bottle from the fridge, popped the cork and poured the bubbling liquid into two tall slender-stemmed glasses. 'To our deal.'

Evie sipped from the glass he handed her and choked as the bubbles flew up her nose. 'Oh—that's—' she coughed '—yummy.' She took another mouthful. 'Happy Christmas. How long do we have to keep this up? When will you know if you've rescued your deal?'

He looked out of the window. 'We've arrived.'

And he hadn't answered her question.

Wondering once again what it was about this particular deal that was so important, Evie followed his gaze and gasped. 'We're at the Natural History Museum.' The famous building was illuminated against the winter night and thousands of tiny sparkling lights had been threaded through the branches of the trees. In front of the building was an ice rink and the whole place had been transformed into a winter paradise. 'I had no idea they held events here.'

'This is a very prestigious fund-raiser.'

'Can we ice skate?'

'Absolutely not.'

'But it's snowing.' Evie leaned forward, captivated by the atmosphere. 'It would be magical. Do you think we'll have a white Christmas?'

'I couldn't care less. Do you want an umbrella?'

'You don't like snow? Seriously?'

'It's useful when I'm skiing. The rest of the time it's an inconvenience.'

'When did you last make a snowman or throw a snowball?'

Rio frowned. 'We need to get out of the car, Evie.'

Evie didn't budge. 'You don't write to Santa, you hate decorations, you don't like snow, you won't ice skate—there must be *something* you like about Christmas. Turkey? Meeting up with friends? What's the best thing about Christmas for you?'

The door was opened by his security chief and a blast of cold air entered the car.

Rio stared at her for a long moment, his face unsmiling. 'The best thing about Christmas for me is when it's over,' he gritted. 'Now, get out of the car and smile.'

'So the rumours are true, Rio? You're engaged? You do realise you've just ruined every single woman's Christmas, and half the married ones, too?' Tabitha Fenton-Coyle stroked her long red fingernails over his sleeve. 'Tell me what it is about her that induced a hardened cynic like yourself into marriage.'

'You need to ask?'

'Well, she's pretty, of course, in a slightly unsophisticated way that a man might find appealing—' There was a flinty glint in Tabitha's eyes and Rio turned his head and noticed Evie laughing uninhibitedly with the two Russian billionaires, both known for their arrogant refusal to speak English at social events. They were taciturn, remote and notoriously unapproachable and yet both appeared to be listening to Evie with rapt attention.

How was she making herself understood?

From across the table, Rio tried to hear what she was saying. She was chatting non-stop, her hands moving as she illustrated her point. Occasionally she paused to sip champagne or listen to their response.

'Clever of you to find a woman who speaks Russian,' Tabitha said, 'given your business interests in that country. Is that how you met? Is she an interpreter or something?'

Evie spoke Russian?

Unable to hear her above the noise from the surrounding tables, Rio focused his gaze on her lips and realised that she was indeed speaking Russian.

His hostess was watching him. 'You didn't know, did you? Well, if she can persuade them to open their wallets when the charity auction begins, then she'll certainly get my vote.'

Where had Evie learned to speak Russian?

Why hadn't she mentioned it when he'd told her that Vladimir didn't speak good English and that she wouldn't be able to communicate without an interpreter? And then he remembered her responding that she wouldn't need an interpreter. At the time he'd assumed she'd meant that she'd be using sign language and lots of smiles—not once had it occurred to him that she spoke fluent Russian.

Coffee was served as the auction began and there was a sudden flurry of movement as people swapped seats.

Her cheeks pink with excitement, Evie swayed to her feet and found her way to the seat next to him. 'I'm having *such* a nice time. Those men are so sweet. You should have mentioned how funny they were.'

Rio tightened his grip on the glass. 'Just as you should possibly have mentioned the fact that you're fluent in Russian.'

'You were being arrogant and I thought it would be more fun to just surprise you. I thought it might teach you not to underestimate people.' Craning her neck, she looked over his shoulder towards the stage and the dance floor. 'What's happening now?'

Rio fingered the stem of his glass. 'I do *not* underestimate people.'

'Yes, you do. But you probably can't help it,' she said kindly. 'Is there going to be dancing?'

'It's the auction first. The bidding will raise money for the charity.' Rio was still watching her. 'Do you speak any other languages?'

'French, Spanish and Mandarin. So am I allowed to bid for something?'

'You speak *four* languages?'

'Five, if you count English. How much am I allowed to bid?'

'You don't speak Italian?'

'No.' She helped herself to a chocolate from the plate. 'That CD was always out of the library whenever I looked.'

Rio shot her an incredulous look. 'You taught yourself all those languages?'

'I'm good at languages. I taught myself the basics and then there was a teacher at school who helped me and I had a friend who spoke Mandarin and Russian.' She was looking across the room. 'Don't look now but there's a huge Christmas tree next to the stage—you'd better close your eyes or it will probably give you a nervous breakdown. I'm surprised you didn't phone ahead and ask them to remove it.'

Still absorbing the fact that she spoke five languages, Rio dragged his gaze to the stage and saw the Christmas tree. She was right; it was huge—a massive symbol of the unspeakable horrors of his childhood. There was a rushing sound in his ears and suddenly the voices around him seemed far away. Instead of staring at glittering baubles, he was staring into a deep, dark black hole. Memories formed pictures in his brain, taking on shapes he didn't want to see, like a gruesome kaleidoscope. That hideous morning. The discovery he'd made. The shock. And the emptiness.

Suddenly every sparkle in the room seemed to intensify the dark feelings swirling in his brain. Every silver star and rope of tinsel was a silent mockery.

Promising himself that they'd leave as soon as the auction was over, Rio sat still, ruthlessly wrestling his feelings back under control.

From inside a fog of unwelcome memories, he was dimly aware of Evie leaning across the table, coaxing the Russians into bidding enormous sums of money in the charity auction. Even Tabitha was looking impressed as Evie switched between Russian and English, extracting more money from the billionaires than they'd sucked oil from the Caspian Sea.

If the circumstances had been different, Rio would have laughed. As it was, he just wanted to leave.

They'd been seen together. The ring had been photographed. Rumours were spreading.

It was done.

Rio watched with a frown as Tabitha made sure that Evie's glass was kept topped up. She was drinking the champagne as if it were soda, and he realised that if he didn't remove her from this table quickly she was going to be drunk.

As the auction ended and a band started warming up on the stage, Rio drained his glass and turned to Evie.

'We're leaving.'

'No way! Not this time. I missed almost all of the film— I'm not missing the rest of the ball. The dancing hasn't started yet.' She started to sway in her seat in time to the music while Tabitha looked on with a mixture of condescension and amusement.

'If you can persuade Rio to dance with you, then I'm willing to believe he's in love. I've never known him to dance. If I didn't know better, I'd think he didn't have rhythm.' She gave Rio a knowing look and he saw Evie's happy smile falter as she digested the meaning behind those words.

Rio cursed silently.

She might be tipsy, but she wasn't so under the influence that she didn't recognise a barb when it was poked into her flesh.

Removing the champagne glass from her hand, he dragged her to her feet. 'You're right—we'll dance.' Without giving himself time to think about it, he led her onto the dance floor and slid his arm around her waist. 'Smile.'

'What is there to smile about? She's flaunting the fact she's had sex with you. She's *vile*. And you have no taste. No wonder you've never wanted to settle down with anyone if she's the sort of person you've been seeing.'

'I have *not* had sex with her,' Rio breathed, bending his head so that he spoke the words in her ear and couldn't be overheard. Immediately, her perfume wound itself round his senses. 'She was trying to cause trouble. Trying to hurt you. Don't let her. You're just over-emotional because you've had too much champagne. Now smile, because the whole purpose of tonight is to convince people our relationship is real.'

'Well, if this relationship were real, I would have punched her. And I'm not over-emotional, I'm justifiably emotional. That woman is a man-eater. She ought to be fenced in on a game reserve. Do you know that she's on her *fourth* husband? Evgeni and Vladimir told me that she only marries them for their money.'

Rio's tension levels rocketed up several more notches. 'You're on first name terms with the Russians?'

'I sat with them all evening, what did you expect? When I saw that awful Tabitha woman had separated us I almost had a heart attack. She put me there thinking I'd struggle, didn't she? She was trying to be unkind.'

Rio gave a faint smile. 'I think you won that round.'

'They told me that she takes men to the cleaners and lives off the settlement.'

'It's a popular career choice in certain circles.'

'Well, I think it's awful. No amount of money would make up for being married to someone I didn't love.' Evie slid her arms around his neck, her eyes slightly bleary. 'I mean, actually, when you think about it, that's not so far from prostitution, is it?'

Conscious of the shocked glances from those nearest to them, Rio smiled. 'Absolutely right,' he purred, vastly entertained by how outspoken she became when she'd had a few glasses of champagne. 'You might want to lower your voice before you cast any more aspersions on the character and profession of our illustrious hostess.'

Evie gulped. 'Oops. Do you think they heard me?'

'Definitely. They're doubtless all now engrossed in a fascinating debate as to whether our hostess is a prostitute or not.'

Evie leaned her forehead against his chest. 'Sorry. I may have drunk just a little bit too much champagne—I've never had it before and it's *delicious*.'

'You've never had champagne before?'

'Never. Last year, Grandpa and I treated ourselves to a bottle of Prosecco but it wasn't the same.'

Rio winced. 'No. It definitely isn't the same. Prosecco is excellent in a Bellini but it's not champagne.' He lifted his hand and removed a strand of fiery red hair that had somehow managed to tangle itself around his bow tie. 'I think I'd better take you home.'

'I don't want to go home. I want to dance. Anyway, I like it here and we're supposed to be seen.' Still clinging to him tightly, she swayed in time to the music and then looked up with a smile as everyone started singing *The Twelve Days of Christmas*.

'Oh, I *love* this. This used to be my party piece at school. I do all the actions. Wait till you see my Seven swans a-swimming—'

Rio inhaled deeply. 'Evie—' But she was already lifting her hands like a conductor, waving her arms and singing at the top of her voice along with everyone else.

'—partridge in a pear tree—'

'I'm taking you home.'

'No.' She dug her heels in like a stubborn horse. 'I'm not going anywhere. I've never been to a party as amazing as this one. I don't want it to end.'

Rio gritted his teeth. 'We have two more to attend tomorrow. And this time I won't make the mistake of giving you champagne beforehand.'

'I don't care about tomorrow. I want to live for today. I like *this* party.' She slid her arms around his neck and pressed herself against him, her breath warm against his neck. 'Please, Rio, dance with me. You know you want to.'

He locked his fingers around her wrists, intending to remove her arms, but then she smiled up at him and he found himself so captivated by that smile that instead of removing her arms, he slid his hands down her warm skin. Her back was bare, her skin warm and smooth and tempting and raw lust shot through him. Without thinking about what he was doing, Rio lowered his mouth towards hers.

'*Four calling birds, three French hens—*'

Rio froze as she started to sing again. 'Evie—'

'*Two turtle doves, and a—*'

'Evie!' Rio felt tension prickle down his spine.

'I like singing. If you want me to stop singing, you're going to have to gag me.'

'Good idea.' Rio closed the distance and captured her mouth with his. The chemistry was instantaneous and explosive. Because he had his hand on her bare back he could feel the tremors that shook her and he welded her closer to him, ignoring the curious looks of those around him.

After two of the most intoxicating, arousing, exciting minutes of his life, he lifted his head fractionally and tried to regain his balance. The kiss had done nothing except make him crave more. He wanted to touch and taste—he wanted to bury his face in her hair and feast on her body.

Around them, everyone was still singing but this time Evie wasn't joining in.

'When you kiss me, I don't ever want it to stop,' she murmured, her eyes slightly glazed. 'It feels incredible. Are you as good at everything else? If so, then it's no wonder every woman in the room is looking at me as if they hate me. They think we're having mad, crazy sex all the time. I wish. Maybe we should. It seems a shame to disappoint everyone.'

He cupped her face in his hands and stared down at her in exasperation. 'You're plastered. It's time I took you home.'

'I'm not plastered. And I don't want to go home. I'm having a really great time and I refuse to go home just so that you can weld yourself to your laptop again and ignore the fact it's Christmas. Kissing you, drinking champagne, dancing and singing—they're my favourite things. Honestly, Rio, you should sing too—it's fun—I'm feeling so *Christmassy*—' Her hips swayed and there was a huge smile on her face as she started to sing along again, joining in with the crowd, this time at double the volume—

When it came to *'Five gold rings'* she sang even louder, struck a dramatic pose and flashed her diamond in the air, beaming at Rio.

Before he could stop her, she flung herself towards the two Russians, kissed each of them on the cheek and then sprang onto a chair and from there onto the table.

Rio closed his eyes, cursing himself for not monitoring her champagne intake more closely. He contemplated removing her bodily but decided that she would probably make such a fuss that the best thing to do was to wait until the end of the song and hope she survived that long without falling off the table and doing herself serious injury.

Everyone was clapping and Evie was by now the centre of attention as she led the singing, her actions for *Seven swans a-swimming* causing such hilarity that Rio shook his head in disbelief.

'She's certainly the life and soul of the party,' Vladimir was suddenly beside him, speaking in slow, broken English, and beaming up at Evie, who was still mimicking a swan. 'That joint venture you wanted to explore in Moscow—we're willing to give it some consideration. Fly over in the New Year and meet with us. Evie can translate for you.'

Rio, who had given up on the usually taciturn Russians, was about to confirm the details when an overenthusiastic re-enactment of *'Three French hens'* almost sent Evie spinning off the table.

'*Scusi*—' Crossing to the table, he caught Evie as she lost her balance and she tumbled into his arms, the silver dress shimmering under the lights.

'—*Two purple doves*,' she hollered, '*and a partridge in a pear tree.*'

Wild applause surrounded them and Rio winced. 'That's your party piece?'

'One of them. I also tell a great joke about a wide mouth toad which has brilliant actions.' She eyed the microphone on the stage. 'I suppose I could—'

'No,' Rio said hastily. 'You most definitely could not.'

'I love champagne,' she said happily, leaning her head against his shoulder. 'It's the nicest, yummiest, fizziest, happiest drink I've ever tasted. Is there any more?'

'It's run out. You drank it all. Thanks to you, the global champagne market is now in meltdown.'

'Shame.' She buried her face in his neck and breathed

deeply. 'You smell so good. Why do you smell so good? Will you kiss me again? And this time don't stop. The only thing I hate about kissing you is when you stop. I just want it to go on and on and on—could you do that, do you think? You did say you were good at multi-tasking.'

Rio tensed. 'Evie—'

'You're an incredibly sexy man. If I wasn't so afraid of being rejected again, I'd try and seduce you—' she was snuggling and kissing his neck at the same time '—but I've never seduced anyone before so it's probably a bit overambitious to start with you. Like climbing a mountain and deciding to start with Everest. I ought to practice on someone small, ugly and unsuccessful first and see how I get on.'

Rio felt his entire body tighten. 'You won't be practising on anyone tonight. We're going home.'

'Not without a present from the Christmas tree,' she coaxed, lifting her head and focusing with difficulty. 'It's all in a good cause. You pay money and they give you a surprise present. The money goes to the kids. So it's sort of two presents in one. Three presents actually, because you get a warm fuzzy feeling from being generous.'

Deciding that it was going to be quicker to buy the present than argue, Rio strode towards the tree, Evie still in his arms. Around them, people were smiling indulgently.

His pulse rate doubled as he approached the tree. The smell of pine invaded his nostrils, awakening thoughts and memories long dormant.

'Which present?' he growled, adjusting the angle of his body so that she could see the tree and he couldn't. 'Tell me which one you want.' Quickly. So that he could make his escape. The past was rolling over him like a dark cloud, its creeping menace threatening to seep under the barriers of his self-control.

'The pink one with the silver bow.' Her arms tightened

around his neck and Rio felt the moist flicker of her tongue against his throat.

'That one—' His voice tight, he indicated with his head towards the pink box and one of the staff untied it from the tree and handed it to him while one of his own security team discreetly dealt with the financial aspect of the transaction.

'Thank you.' Her voice was husky, her mouth tantalizingly close to his and Rio tried to ignore the perfume that wafted from her skin.

'We're going home.'

'So that we can experiment with fur against naked flesh?'

Jaw clenched tight, he reminded himself that she dreamed of happy endings.

If there was one thing designed to kill his libido, it was a woman who dreamed of happy endings.

'So that you can sleep off the champagne.'

'Wait—' Slightly breathless, she pressed her lips against his throat. 'I want the tree. Will you buy me the tree?'

Rio stilled. 'You want me to buy every present on the tree?'

'No, I want you to buy me the *tree*. I don't think I can stand the thought of Christmas without a tree. It's like having chocolate cake with no chocolate.' Still clutching the pink box, she snuggled against him, her voice coaxing. 'That tree would look fantastic in the Penthouse. It's even bigger than the one I decorated.'

The one he'd had removed.

'I don't want a tree.'

'Why not? I know you prefer to work over Christmas, but it isn't going to stop you working just because there's a tree in the room. It cheers everything up.'

'It doesn't cheer me up.'

She frowned. 'So it wasn't my decorations in particular that you didn't like. It's Christmas trees in general. Why?

You're never too old to enjoy Christmas. Having a tree will give you happy memories.'

Rio put her down so suddenly she staggered. 'I don't have any happy memories of Christmas.'

It was the stricken look in her eyes that made him realise just how harshly he'd spoken. 'I...I'm sorry,' she stammered. 'I didn't mean—'

'Forget it. Let's get out of here.'

CHAPTER SIX

I don't have any happy memories of Christmas.

Evie sat in the middle of the enormous bed, those words reverberating around her head. She'd put her foot in it, but knowing that didn't stop her wondering and asking herself endless questions.

Why didn't he have happy memories of Christmas?

She turned her head and looked towards the double doors that lay between her and the sitting room. They remained firmly closed.

What was he doing? Had he gone to sleep in the second bedroom?

They'd driven home without speaking, Evie silenced by that one revealing phrase and Rio communicating nothing. For once, his BlackBerry was silent and he'd simply stared out of the window at the snowy streets, his handsome face an expressionless mask.

But he *was* feeling, she knew that.

Not just feeling—*hurting*.

Knowing that she was risking another rejection, Evie slid off the bed and opened the doors quietly, afraid to disturb him if he was sleeping.

The huge living room was in darkness. The flames of the fire had almost flickered to nothing and all the lights had been extinguished.

He wasn't there.

She was overreacting. He'd obviously chosen to sleep in the second bedroom.

Evie was about to turn and go back to bed when she noticed a ghostly green glow in the corner of the room and realised that it was the laptop screen.

As her eyes slowly adjusted to the darkness, she saw that Rio was seated at the table.

'It's four in the morning,' she murmured. 'You should get some sleep.'

'I'm not tired.' His voice was barely audible. 'Go back to bed, Evie. Sleep it off.'

Knowing that she was unwelcome, she was about to do just that but her feet froze to the spot as her eyes adjusted to the dim light and she managed to make out his profile. He looked like a man on the edge. A man struggling to contain an emotion bigger than him.

He was still looking at the screen, but somehow she knew that this time he wasn't reading the numbers. His eyes were bleak and empty and she knew instantly that this was about Christmas.

I don't have any happy memories of Christmas.

What sort of childhood had he had, that he hadn't retained a single happy memory of Christmas?

The sudden stillness of the room seemed loud in her ears.

Evie stood still, knowing that she was intruding on a private moment. She knew she ought to back away and return to the neutral sanctuary of the bedroom. She ought to close those big doors and leave him to his dark thoughts. She was never going to see him again once this charade was over. Why did it even matter that he wanted to shut himself away and pretend Christmas wasn't happening?

But there was something about the bleak set of his features that made it impossible for her to walk away. She never would have been able to walk away and leave another human being in so much pain, and she had no doubt that he was in pain.

She'd become intimately acquainted with the signs after her grandmother had died. Night after night, she'd seen the same look on her grandfather's face as he'd sat in her grandmother's favourite rocking chair, just staring at her photograph. She'd kept him company in the darkness, afraid to leave him alone with his grief.

What had Rio Zaccarelli lost?

What was he thinking about, as he stared sightlessly at that screen?

Evie walked across to him, knowing that she was taking a risk. She was approaching when she should have run away.

Rio lifted his head and inhaled deeply. 'I said, go back to bed.'

'My head spins when I lie down.'

'You drank too much champagne. That feeling will pass. Drink lots of water.'

'I'm not drunk.'

The barest flicker of a smile touched his mouth. 'You were dancing on the table.'

'That wasn't because I was drunk. It was because I'd lost some of my inhibitions. If I had the confidence, I would have done the same thing sober. The drink just made me less anxious.'

'In that case, remind me never to escort you when you're drunk.'

'Tell me why you hate Christmas.'

Anger flickered across his face and his swift glance was loaded with warning. 'I think you should go to bed.'

'Only if you come too.' She had no idea what had driven her to say those words. Immediately, she wanted to drag them back. *What if he said yes?* She'd never had a one-night stand in her life. Compared with his experience and sophistication, she was a complete novice.

For a moment he simply watched her, his eyes glittering in the darkness. She had the feeling that he was fighting some brutal internal battle.

'Leave,' he said thickly. 'Right now.'

'I'm not drunk.'

'That isn't why I want you to leave.'

'Then—'

'I'm fresh out of happy endings, Evie. You won't find one within a thousand kilometres of me.'

Her mouth dried and her heart was pounding in her chest. 'I know that. You could never be my happy ending. But that doesn't mean...I want to know...'

His eyes were hard and unsympathetic. He gave her no help at all. 'What do you want to know, Evie?'

She licked dry lips. 'I want to know what it would be like,' she whispered. 'If the rest of it would feel as good as the kissing part.'

'You want to know how it would feel?' He rose to his feet so suddenly that she actually took an involuntary step backwards and he registered her retreat with a sardonic smile. 'I'll tell you how it would feel, Evie. It would feel good. We've both felt the chemistry. It would be incredible. Hot and crazy. For a short time.' His voice was thickened by emotion. 'And then I'd break your heart. Like that—' He snapped his fingers in a cruel, casual gesture that made her flinch. 'Easy.'

The blood was pulsing in her ears and it was difficult to breathe. 'That's fine.'

His gaze mocked. 'You're saying it's fine for me to break your heart?'

'No. I'm saying you won't break it. To break it, I'd have to be in love with you and I'm not in love with you. I wouldn't be that stupid.'

His lids lowered, half concealing black eyes that glittered dark and dangerous. 'Perhaps I'm not in the mood for a gentle seduction.'

Evie felt a spasm of fear, intermingled with the most fierce excitement she'd ever experienced. It was like a drug, urging her on to be more and more daring. 'If you're trying to scare me, you're not succeeding.'

'Maybe you should be scared, Evie.' His voice was lethally soft and cold as the ice that had formed on the windows. 'I'm not the right man for you.'

'I know that.' They were alone in the room and yet she was whispering. 'That isn't what this is about.'

'So what is it about? What are you trying to prove to yourself? Or is this good girl seduces bad boy, just to see how it feels?'

'No! I—' Evie broke off, struggling to breathe. 'I don't know what this is. All I know is…I thought you wanted… earlier you said…'

'I know what I said. I know what I wanted.'

'So—'

'Earlier, I didn't know what I was dealing with.'

Evie flushed. 'Because I love Christmas and believe in happy endings? I said I didn't believe in happy endings with you.'

His eyes held hers. 'If you play with fire, you'll get burnt.'

'Will you tell me why you hate Christmas?'

'No. And you're making this personal. A basic female mistake.'

'All right. Nothing personal. No questions.' Part of her was shocked at herself. What was she doing?

'You think you can go to bed with a man and not make it personal?' There was a layer of humour in his voice. 'You think you can do that?'

'Yes.' *No.* She had no idea.

Rio stared at her for a long moment and then lifted his hand and took a strand of her hair in his fingers. 'You should be more careful with yourself, Evie Anderson. You could get seriously hurt.' The backs of his fingers brushed her cheek and Evie shivered, dazed by the spark of electricity that shot through her body.

Her heart pounding, she turned her head and ran her tongue along his fingers.

His response was instantaneous. With a growl, he cupped her face in his hands and brought his mouth down on hers in a punishing, possessive kiss. He'd kissed her before, but this kiss was different. This kiss demanded everything and Evie felt all her senses ignite with explosive force. Within an instant she was light-headed, her limbs weak and wobbly.

With a moan, she slid her hands up his chest, over his shoulders, feeling the firm swell of muscle beneath her hands. He'd discarded his bow tie and undone the first few buttons of his shirt and her fingers slid inside, seeking, touching, exploring. She felt the pulsing heat of his body beneath her fingertips and made a small, desperate sound deep in her throat and then he was kissing her again and his tongue was hot against hers, his relentless seduction so much more prac- tised than her own desperate offering.

The kiss seemed to last for ever and she felt her entire body stir, as if it had been waiting for this exact moment to come alive. And the feelings were so intense that it was impossible to stay silent.

When he pressed his mouth to the hollow of her throat she moaned, and when he dragged his mouth lower and toyed with the straining peak of her breast she arched her back and gasped his name. She wanted more, much more, and when he closed his hand over the hem of her nightdress she didn't stop him. There was a tearing sound as he ripped it from neck to hem and then she was naked, her body visible in the warm glow of the firelight.

If she'd thought that the semi darkness might give her some protection, she was wrong. Rio drew away from her, his breathing audible as he scanned her body, his gaze lingering on the fiery red curls that nestled at the juncture of her thighs.

'You can still change your mind.'

'No.' Emotion clogged her throat and the only thing in her head was a desperate need for this man. 'I don't want to change my mind.'

His fingers speared her hair and tightened, drawing her head back. His eyes were fierce, black and focused—focused on her.

For a few suspended seconds she didn't breathe and then he seemed to make a decision. Without speaking, he clamped his hand behind her head and claimed her mouth with ravenous hunger. It was a full on assault, his tongue in her mouth, his kiss blatantly sexual and brutally erotic and Evie went from freezing to boiling in a microsecond, her body burning up under the heat of his. She ripped at his shirt, clawing, tearing in a desperate attempt to get to the sleek male flesh beneath. Finally his shirt dangled open at the front and her hands slid inside and up to his shoulders. His body was a work of art, his muscles pumped up and hard, the dark shading on his chest accentuating strength and masculinity. Desperate to taste, Evie pushed at his chest and they rolled. Now he was the one on his back, his eyes glittering dark in the firelight as he watched her. Then his hand moved behind her head and he brought her mouth down to his, kissing her hungrily as her hair tumbled between them. Evie kissed him back, matching his hunger with her own, her hands sliding over his body as she straddled him. For a moment she paused, her hair tumbling around them, her senses reaching overload. His eyes were dark, so dark, and she felt an overwhelming thrill of excitement as she felt him, hard and ready beneath her. In that single moment, her breath caught. It was like reaching the top of a roller coaster and realising that there was no turning back.

'You're shaking—' His voice was raw and thickened

with the same passion she was feeling. 'Do you want me to stop?'

'No,' she whispered. She leaned forward so that her mouth brushed his. 'I can't stop. I want this more than anything. I want *you*.'

'Why?'

She sensed his struggle to hold back. It was visible in his eyes and in the tension of his sleek, pumped muscles.

'Does it matter?' Her mouth was against his. 'It feels right. Can't that be enough?'

He didn't answer her question. Instead, he closed his hands over her hips and lifted her, flipping her gently onto her back, once more the aggressor as he came over her. The outside world melted away. Details blurred. Dimly, Evie registered that he was now naked and that brief glimpse was enough to send nerves licking along the edges of her excitement.

He devoured her mouth and she kissed him back, every bit as hungry for him as he very clearly was for her.

The heat was shocking, an inferno of dangerous desire and carnal craving and, when he dragged his mouth from her lips to her neck, Evie sucked in air and tried to focus. But there was nothing to hold on to except him. Her whole world was tumbling around her and he was the only solid thing remaining. When his hand slid between her thighs she moaned against his mouth and he murmured something in Italian, his clever fingers sliding skilfully against delicate flesh. He knew exactly where to touch her, *how to touch her,* and Evie felt the ache in her body intensify until it was almost agonizing. She shifted her hips on the rug, whimpered his name, but Rio simply watched her, his mouth only a breath away from hers as he tormented her with merciless skill.

'Please,' Evie begged, arching towards him, 'Please, Rio—'

As if something snapped inside him, he shifted onto her.

He stroked her hair away from her face and scanned her features with eyes that were dark with secrets.

She felt the hardness of him brush against her and tensed. 'Please—' In desperation, she ran her hands down his body and her heart gave a little lurch as she touched the power of him.

He leaned his forehead against hers, holding her gaze. 'I don't want to hurt you—'

'You won't.'

There was a brief pause while he protected her and then he was inside her, hard and hot. The size of him shocked her and Evie forced herself to relax as she learned to accommodate him.

'Breathe—' His voice was husky and he lowered his mouth to hers. 'Breathe, *tesoro*.'

'Can't—' Her body was on fire and he gently brushed her mouth with his, tracing her lower lip with his tongue as he eased deeper.

She felt an agonizing flash of pain, immediately followed by excitement as he moved against sensitive flesh and she dug her nails hard into his back, feeling the tension shimmering in his powerful frame.

He was holding back. *Holding back for her.*

Her heart was pounding, her cheeks were flushed and her blood raced with every agonizingly slow stroke. Pleasure streaked through her and she cried out his name, telling him how much she wanted him, how much she needed him and he answered with his body, driving into her with controlled force, attacking her senses with a savage sensuality.

The storm inside was fierce and furious, raging through her like a wild beast, ready to burn up everything it touched. What they shared was primitive and elemental and she knew deep down in the very fibre of her being that nothing was ever going to be the same again.

She felt his fingers dig hard into the soft flesh of her thigh and then faster, harder, he built the rhythm until there was nothing in her head but a thundering roar, until everything inside and around her shattered into a million tiny fragments and she fell, spinning and tumbling, into a different world.

When she woke, she was alone in the bed. At some point during the early hours he'd transferred her to the bedroom, tucking her under the soft duvet. She had a vague recollection of pleading with him to join her and an equally vague recollection that his response to her request had been to pull away and return to the living room, making good on his earlier warning that their intimacies would be physical, not emotional. He'd returned to his laptop—to his own silent world. A world that didn't include Christmas or people.

A world that didn't include her.

Dizzy with lack of sleep, her body aching in unusual places, Evie slid out of the bed, blushing as she realised her nightdress was probably still lying in pieces on the floor of the living room.

So this was how it felt to sleep with a man you weren't in love with.

Padding across the thickly carpeted floor, she gazed in the mirror at herself, trying to see the differences. Same blue eyes. Same freckles. Same crazy morning hair.

She looked the same. Outwardly, nothing had changed. Maybe she could live a life that included sex without happy endings. Other women did it all the time. Maybe she could too.

Hearing his voice from the living room, Evie quickly pulled on a robe and followed the sound. He was on the phone, talking to someone in a time zone more alive than theirs. He'd made love to her for most of the night, but that hadn't stopped him working. Nothing stopped him working. But now she was wondering whether work was a refuge rather than a goal. A place to escape rather than a strategy for global domination.

The first thing she saw when she entered the room were newspapers stacked on the low table between the sofas.

Her stomach lurched and she felt sick with apprehension.

This was it. This was the moment she'd been dreading. This was the reason for the charade.

Had they printed that horribly revealing photograph?

Was that why he was on the telephone?

Hardly daring to look, she sank onto the sofa and stared at the newspaper on top of the pile, forcing herself to breathe slowly. It was one of the tabloids. If anyone had printed the picture of her naked, surely it would be them. Her hand shaking, she reached out and lifted it onto her lap. The headlines blurred and suddenly she didn't want to look, as if postponing the moment could alter the outcome.

'*Calma, tesoro.* It's all right.' His voice was deep and firm. 'They printed a lovely picture of you with your arms around my neck. The caption is "Tycoon tumbles" or something equally unimaginative. I expect your grandfather will be satisfied with it.'

What did he mean by that? 'So you were right.' Even though he'd reassured her, her fingers were damp with sweat as she forced herself to turn the pages. 'Because we gave them another photo opportunity and a bigger story, they used that instead. Thank you.' The relief was almost painful. 'Thank you so much.' Her eyes glistened as she looked up at him. 'I don't know what I would have done if they'd used that photograph. I'm so grateful to you.'

A muscle flickered in his jaw. 'You have no reason to be grateful to me, Evie.'

'Yes, I have. It was your idea to give them a better story. I would have tried to pay them off and that never would have worked because I suppose they would have just kept coming back for more money.'

He drew his hand over the back of his neck and she saw the muscles in his forearm flex, revealing a tension she didn't understand. 'Evie—'

'You don't have to say anything,' she said hastily. 'I do realise that this is just one day and that they could use that photograph tomorrow, but I'm not going to think about that now. We'll take it a day at a time. Maybe we can make sure they take another photograph of us tonight. Keep giving them something else to print. I promise not to dance on the table again, no matter how Christmassy I feel. What are our plans?'

He didn't answer immediately and she turned her attention back to the newspaper, turning the pages until she found the photograph. 'It's big. I had no idea they'd be that interested.' And she saw instantly why he'd made that comment about her grandfather liking the photograph. She was in Rio's arms, smiling up at him, looking completely smitten. No one looking at that picture would have questioned the authenticity of their relationship. A strange feeling twisted in the pit of her stomach. Was that really the way she'd looked at him? Had he noticed? 'We look good. They were obviously convinced.'

'Champagne certainly brings out an interesting side to you,' he drawled softly and she glanced up to find his eyes on her face.

'I really wasn't drunk.'

'But you were a virgin.'

Fire rose in her cheeks and she sat in silence for a moment, trying to find the right response. 'So what?'

'Why didn't you tell me?'

Was that the reason for his tension? Was it simply the fact that she was so much less experienced than him? 'Well, it isn't exactly something that comes up in conversation,' she said lightly, 'and I don't see that it matters. You wanted someone wholesome. If the press choose to dig around in my past they won't find anything. Isn't that what you wanted?' She kept noticing small things about him—like the bold curve of his eyebrows and the cluster of dark hairs revealed by the open neck of his shirt. Knowing what she knew now, she could easily picture the rest of his body—his chest shadowed with the same dark hair, concealing well defined muscle and breathtaking power. Knowing what she knew, everything was different. More sharply defined, more acutely felt.

The unspoken sexual component to their relationship had been there from the first moment they'd met but it had been enhanced a thousand times by the intimacies they'd shared in the flickering glow of firelight.

'You told me you were engaged.'

'I was.'

'But you didn't have a physical relationship?' His tone was incredulous.

'If you saw the house where I grew up, you wouldn't find it so surprising.' Evie pushed her hair away from her face with a hand that wasn't quite steady. 'I was all set to go to university, but after my grandmother died I couldn't bear to leave my grandfather on his own. I got a job in the village and went to night school to study languages. Jeff and I started dating because we were the only two people under fifty in the village. There was no way I was going to have sex in Grandpa's house. Even if it had been possible, it wouldn't have felt right.'

'Presumably, you didn't conduct your entire relationship with your grandfather looking on. There must have been *some* moments when you were alone.'

'Yes, I suppose there were—' Evie hesitated. 'But neither of us...we didn't really... Honestly, I think we were just friends. We should never have been anything else but I think we were swept along by the expectations of everyone around us.'

'Friends?' His dark brows locked in a puzzled frown and she smiled, thinking how much she'd learned about him in such a short time.

'I bet you've never been friends with a woman in your life, have you?'

'If by "friends" you mean no sex, then the answer is no. So you were engaged, but you never had sex.'

'I don't think either of us was in any hurry.'

'You were in a hurry last night,' he said silkily. 'Or was the champagne to blame for your sudden transformation from virgin to vamp?'

She sucked in a breath, mortified at his blatant reminder of her own desperation. 'No,' she said softly. 'It was you.'

'Let's test that theory, shall we?' He drew her to her feet and a thrill of expectation shot through her.

'Now?'

'Was it the champagne, Evie?' He murmured the words against her mouth and her eyes closed, her heart racing crazily as she rose on her toes and slid her arms around his neck. He slid his hands down her back and pressed her into him, his kiss tasting of hunger and passion.

Evie opened her mouth under his, matching his erotic demands with her own. Dimly, she registered that she shouldn't be feeling this way. They'd made love for most of the night and yet the fierce hunger inside her was as acute as if they hadn't ever touched. She was greedy for more of what they'd shared.

Rio pushed the robe down her arms with confident hands and the silky fabric slid over her hips and pooled on the floor, leaving her naked.

'It's daylight—' Evie could feel her face burning and he gave a slow smile as he tightened his hands on her shoulders and moved her away from him slightly.

'I know.'

'Stop staring at me,' she muttered. 'You've been with so many seriously beautiful women—'

'And none have excited me the way you do,' he said huskily, sweeping her into his arms and carrying her into the bedroom. 'You have the most incredible body.'

'You only think that because you're tall—and strong, which is why you can carry me without putting your back out—'

'You are extremely slender—' he lowered her onto the mattress '—most of your weight is your breasts and your astonishingly long legs and I have no complaints about either so you have no reason to be shy.' He stripped off his shirt and came down beside her in a fluid movement. 'I've never been with a woman as inexperienced as you—'

'I think I prefer the word "wholesome".' Her confidence faltered. 'Is it a problem?'

'No. It's a complete turn-on. But I'm probably going to shock you.' His dark eyes held hers for a moment and then he gently brushed away a strand of hair from her forehead with the tips of his fingers. 'I'm going to teach you everything you don't know, *tesoro*.'

The brief flicker of trepidation was swiftly transformed into breathless excitement as he kissed his way across her jaw and down her body to her exposed breasts. When he fastened his mouth over one straining peak the pleasure shafted through her and when his skilled fingers toyed with the other the torment rose to screaming pitch.

By the time he eventually pushed her thighs apart she was writhing against the sheets, the excitement ripping through her body like a vicious storm.

With no concession to the bright rays of sun spotlighting the room, Rio parted her with gentle fingers, placed his mouth against her and proceeded to subject her to the most extreme degree of erotic torture. With infinite skill, he explored her with tongue and fingers until Evie was on fire, her whole body burning in the flames he'd created. Tortured by the heat, she tried to move her hips to relieve the unbearable ache but he pinned her flat with his free hand, channelling the whole erotic experience into that one molten part of her until there was nothing in her world but him and the feelings he created.

Overwhelmed, she writhed and sobbed. 'Please—oh— how can you do those things at the same time—?'

He gave a husky laugh. 'I told you I was good at multi-tasking—'

Out of her mind with desire, Evie barely registered the fact that he was now above her before he sank into her with a single possessive thrust that filled her completely. The force and power of him stretched her sensitive flesh and she immediately shot into a climax so intense, so exquisitely agonizing, that her nails dug hard into the sleek muscle of his shoulder as her body convulsed around his.

He captured her mouth, kissing her with erotic intent as he slowly built the rhythm again, driving them both back towards that same peak. And this time, when she tumbled, she took him with her and he kept his mouth on hers, sharing every cry and every gasp, their bodies locked together in a shimmering heat created by the intensity of their own passion.

CHAPTER SEVEN

'YOU'RE insatiable. It's been more than a week—you should be bored with me by now.' Laughing, Evie rolled onto her stomach and leaned on Rio's chest. 'Aren't you ever tired?'

He watched her from beneath lowered lids, his gaze slumberous and unmistakably sexual. 'No. I find sex with you incredibly energizing.'

'So that's how you manage to work such long hours—'

'You should be grateful for that,' he said huskily. 'Otherwise, you wouldn't be getting any sleep at all, *tesoro.*'

'It's only two days until Christmas. You shouldn't be working.' Sometimes, when she woke in the dark, she discovered that he wasn't in bed with her. On one occasion she'd tiptoed sleepily from the bed to find him and discovered him working on the laptop, his gaze fixed intently on the ghostly green glow of the screen.

'I don't need much sleep. I had a few hours.' He slid his hand into her hair, pulled her head down and kissed her. 'Ready for breakfast?'

Evie felt a flutter of nerves in her stomach. Breakfast and mornings meant one thing to her. 'Have the newspapers arrived yet?'

He frowned. 'I have no idea and I don't care.'

'*I* care—I keep thinking about that stupid, horrid photograph.' The mood punctured, she rolled onto her back and stared up at the ceiling.

'Forget it.' Rio shifted over her in a smooth movement, his weight pressing her into the mattress. 'Yesterday they took photographs of you in the front row of the charity fashion show—they'll use one of those. Not one of you naked.'

'But you don't know that for sure—' She felt the sudden tension emanating from his powerful frame.

'I do. You need to trust me.'

Reasoning that he knew a great deal more about the media than she did, Evie forced herself to relax. 'OK. I trust you. But you *do* care, you know you do. That's why we're doing all this. You're worried about your deal going through. Is that still all right? I mean—' Suddenly she felt awkward asking. He didn't talk about stuff, did he? 'I know you don't talk about it but you're always on the phone and I can tell you're stressed about it.'

'I'm not stressed.' Only moments before he'd been relaxed. Now he was frighteningly detached, his handsome face an expressionless mask. 'And everything is fine.'

She shouldn't have asked. 'Good. Whatever it is must be worth a lot for you to care about it so much.'

'Yes. It's worth a lot.' Without warning, he sprang from the bed and prowled towards the bathroom. 'I'm going to take a shower. Order yourself some breakfast.'

His casual dismissal chilled her and Evie pulled the duvet over her naked body, feeling vulnerable and exposed. One minute they were incredibly close—the next, he shut her out.

Listening to the sound of the shower, she wondered what it was about this particular deal that was so important to him. She wished again she'd never raised the subject. Why was he so touchy? Was he worrying about it, or was it just that he didn't like talking about it?

She used the second bathroom to shower and change and was relieved when he joined her for breakfast.

Watching him cautiously, gauging his mood, Evie helped herself to a bowl of fruit. 'I checked the papers. You were right—they printed the photo from the fashion show.'

He poured himself a coffee. 'And what was the head-line?'

Evie blushed. 'Something stupid.' She wondered if he minded the media preoccupation with his love life but Rio simply smiled.

'The world appears to be revelling in my rapid and ex-tremely public conversion from never to forever. We're obvi-ously very convincing, *tesoro*.'

Captivated by that smile, Evie felt her breath catch and her heart gave a dangerous lurch. They were so convincing that she was starting to believe it herself. If it weren't for his occasional moments of icy detachment, it would have been frighteningly easy to forget that this wasn't real. *That some day soon he was going to expect her to dump him.*

Reminding herself to live in the moment, she ate a spoon-ful of fruit. 'We'd better make sure we give them something even more interesting to photograph today then. What are we doing tonight?'

'We have been invited by the Russians to watch a per-formance of the Bolshoi Ballet at the Royal Opera House at Covent Garden.'

'Wow.' Evie licked her spoon. 'I've never been to the ballet. That's really exciting!'

'Is it? I confess that men in tights don't excite me one little bit.' Rio rose to his feet as his phone rang. 'But, given that you're their new best friend and you speak fluent Russian, I'm sure we can make some use of the evening. Excuse me—I need to take this.'

'Of course.' Basking in the heady knowledge that she was useful to him, Evie felt a rush of pleasure that lasted through the day and the evening. She adored the ballet, was in awe of the elegant grandeur of the world famous Opera House and enjoyed acting as interpreter.

Vladimir was as charming to her as ever, but it was Rio who drew her attention. Cocooned in the private box, under the protection of darkness, she found herself looking at him every other second, her eyes drawn to the perfect symmetry of his arrogant features, fatally fascinated by the breathtaking power and masculinity stamped in every angle of his body.

Once, he caught her looking and raised an eyebrow in silent question. Evie simply smiled, relieved to be able to hide her fascination behind the charade of their 'relationship'. That was what she was supposed to do, wasn't it? She was supposed to look.

Again, the photographers were out in force, stealing photographs at every opportunity, but Evie felt nothing but relief because she knew by now that, providing they managed to get an interesting shot, they were unlikely to use the one she dreaded appearing.

They went from the ballet to another ball and this time Rio needed no persuasion to dance with her. His hand was warm on her bare back as they moved together, the rhythm of their bodies perfectly in tune after so many hours spent locked in intimacy.

'You're not singing tonight?' He murmured the words against her lips and Evie reminded herself that it was essential to breathe or she'd fall over. But, when he held her like this, she felt as though everything inside her was suspended.

No wonder no woman had ever dumped him.

He was so insanely gorgeous, who in their right mind would not want to be with him?

'No singing. They've already had that picture.' Her arms were locked around his neck and she could feel the heat of his body against hers. 'Grandpa liked it, by the way—he said it reminded him of last year when I did the same thing at the village hall.'

'You danced on the table?'

'No—fortunately, they didn't have champagne.' She smiled up at him. 'I'd love to do something really Christmassy. Can we go ice skating? I really envied those people skating when we were at the ball. Or maybe we could go and sing Christmas carols. I noticed an invitation for a celebrity carol concert at St Paul's Cathedral—are we going to that? I know you see Christmas as nothing more than an interruption in your working day, but I love this time of year.'

He didn't answer. At first, she thought he hadn't heard her question and Evie was about to open her mouth and ask again when she saw his eyes. It was like staring into a dark pool, knowing that beneath the still, glassy surface lay nothing but danger.

She shivered.

They'd stopped dancing. Stopped moving. Among the streamers and balloons, the people laughing, dancing and singing, they alone stood still, locked in the small private bubble they'd formed for themselves. Evie felt frozen and she thought absently that there was no reason to be cold when the room was so warm, but then she realised that the chill came from him. His skin was cold to touch, his eyes reflecting not celebration but an acute and bitter pain.

'Rio?' She spoke his name softly. She had no idea what was wrong, but she wanted to help and not just because of what they'd shared. She would have felt the same way about anyone who was suffering as much as he clearly was. 'Are you—' She broke off, frustrated with herself. What was she planning to say? *Are you all right?* Well, obviously, the answer to that was a resounding *no,* but he was hardly likely to tell her that, was he? He was the most fiercely private man she'd ever met.

And yet they must be conspicuous, standing there locked

together but not moving, like some elaborate sculpture of lovers.

Evie placed her hand on his cheek, alarmed by how cold he was. 'Shall we go?'

Finally, he seemed to hear her and he stared down at her blankly, as if he'd forgotten she was there. 'Yes,' he said at last. 'I think that would be a good idea.'

Aware that their behaviour was starting to draw curious glances, Evie stood on tiptoe and kissed him gently on the mouth. *Tomorrow's photograph,* she thought as a camera flashed and a woman sighed with envy.

It was snowing again outside and Evie sat quietly in the limousine as it moved silently through the white streets. Normally snow soothed her, but tonight nothing could ease the tension in the car.

She wanted to know what was going on in his head, but she also knew that he wouldn't want to tell her.

After a moment's hesitation, she reached across and took his hand in hers, oddly pleased when he didn't immediately withdraw his.

Once, during the silent journey, she sneaked a glance at his taut profile but he stared sightlessly into the winter night, apparently oblivious to everything except his own thoughts.

After a silent ride in the elevator, they stepped into the Penthouse and immediately the phone calls started.

So that was it?

Whatever menace lurked beneath the surface had apparently been ruthlessly repressed once more.

Evie stood awkwardly, hovering, while he took one phone call and then another before eventually deciding that she might as well go to bed and wait for him there. She had no expectation that he'd join her this time, but he did—at three in the morning, long after she'd ended her silent vigil.

This time there was no gentle seduction, no talking—just wild, out of control sex that blew her mind.

It was only afterwards, when his side of the bed had long grown cold, that she wondered what he'd been trying to escape. Because he had been trying to escape, of that she was sure. The raw, ruthless passion they'd shared hadn't been energizing sex, it had been oblivion sex.

She had to talk to him.

No one who felt that bad should suffer alone.

Feeling distinctly strange, Evie moved quietly into the living room. How did you approach a man you had wild, crazy sex with but no relationship? What were you supposed to say? Technically, were they friends now?

He had his back to her and he was talking in a low voice, his long fingers toying with a sleek, expensive pen.

She was so busy working out what she was going to say when he finished on the phone that it was a moment or two before she actually paid attention to his conversation.

It was his tone that made her listen. The hardness was tempered by something she hadn't heard in his voice before. There was no hint of the ruthless businessman, or the primitive lover. He was infinitely gentle and it was obvious that the person on the other end of the phone meant a lot to him.

More than a lot.

'Sì tesoro—ti amo.'

Evie froze. *Ti amo.* She didn't speak much Italian but she knew that meant *I love you*. Unable to help herself, she listened to the rest of the conversation and picked up a few more words. This man, who claimed not to believe in happy endings, was telling someone that he loved her. That he hoped to see her soon.

The scent of him still clung to her skin, as did hers to him, no doubt, and yet he was already making plans to see another woman.

Her skin felt icy-cold.

She'd slept with another woman's man.

Was this the secret that simmered beneath the surface? Was this the reason for his pain?

Nausea rose in her stomach and her legs felt as though they'd been turned to water.

She'd had sex with a man who was deeply involved with someone else.

Angry with him but even more angry with herself, Evie was about to move when he turned his head and saw her.

'Evie?' His voice was deep and male, surprisingly normal after the emotional tightrope they'd walked the previous night. 'You're awake early. I didn't see you there.'

'Don't worry about it.' She stood stiff, shivering slightly, feeling slightly detached from her surroundings. 'I'm going to get dressed. Then I'm going.'

He frowned. 'Going where?'

'I don't know.' Her shocked mind was paralysed. It refused to provide her with the words and the thoughts she needed to move forward. 'Anywhere but here.'

His eyes hardened. 'We made a deal. It would be catastrophic if you left now. I need you to stay.'

'Why? What's the point of this charade when you're already involved with someone else?' Emotion thickened her voice and she hated herself for not being the cool, rational person she wanted to be. She wanted to be sophisticated enough to thank him for a perfect no-strings-attached relationship and walk away. Instead, she wanted to claw his flawless features and thump him. She wanted him to hurt the way she was hurting. 'Does she know? Does she know about me?'

A muscle flickered in his cheek and he put his pen down, the movement slow and deliberate. 'You were listening to my phone call.'

'Not intentionally. And if you're expecting me to apologise for eavesdropping on a private conversation then forget it. There are some things that shouldn't be private.'

'*Calma*. Calm down.'

'No, I will not *calma* or calm down! I don't speak much Italian, Rio, but I speak enough to understand the gist of what you just said to her! I'm really astonished you've never been dumped if that's the way you treat women. You're right—you are a complete and utter bastard. This whole week we... you...' She broke off, trying to control herself. 'How could you do that? How could you do those things when you're in love with someone else? I thought you were a free agent—single. You should have *told* me you were involved with someone.'

'I'm not involved.'

Her breathing was shallow. 'When you warned me that you'd break my heart, I didn't expect it to happen quite this quickly.'

'Evie—'

'No! Just don't make pathetic excuses, OK? I don't want to hear them. I heard you! I *heard* you talking to your girlfriend.'

He swore softly in Italian and turned away from her.

For a moment, staring at the rigid tension in those broad shoulders, she thought he wasn't even going to bother defending himself.

And then he turned, a savage look on his face. 'You did *not* hear me talking to my girlfriend. It wasn't a woman.' His voice was raw and Evie stood still, frozen to the spot by the look in his eyes.

'But—'

'You heard me talking to a child. She's four years old. A child, not a woman. My daughter.' He let out a long breath. 'You heard me talking to my daughter.'

'All right. Keep me informed.' Rio terminated the conversation with his lawyer and looked up to see Evie standing there. She'd changed into a pair of jeans and a blue cashmere jumper. Her hair, still damp from the shower, accentuated the extreme pallor of her face.

'Why didn't you tell me you have a child?' Her voice was flat. 'Why didn't you mention it?'

Programmed to keep women at a distance, Rio kept his response cool. 'It isn't any of your business.' Seeing the hurt in her eyes, he wished he hadn't been quite so blunt. 'I don't talk about my private life. To anyone.'

'I'm not some journalist, Rio!' She swept her hand through her hair, her confusion evident in every movement she made. 'We slept together, for God's sake. We shared—'

'Sex,' Rio drawled. 'We shared sex. A physical relationship, however satisfying, doesn't give you access to the rest of my life. Don't make the mistake of thinking that it does.'

Her head jerked as if he'd slapped her and for a moment he thought she was going to do exactly that to him. Instead, she lost still more colour from her cheeks and nodded stiffly. 'Of course it doesn't. My mistake. You have a child. Forgive me for thinking that's something you might have mentioned.' She turned away from him and stalked towards the table that had already been laid for breakfast. 'Are those today's papers?' Her hands shook as she lifted one and flicked through it. 'Have they used the photograph? Or haven't you bothered to check? I'm worried we didn't give them much of interest last night.'

She was rigidly polite and Rio watched her in silence, knowing that he was going to have to tell her the truth and wondering why that felt like a difficult conversation. He'd done what needed to be done. In the same circumstances, he'd make all the same decisions. *So why did he feel so uncomfortable?* 'They haven't used it. They have, however, printed the one they took when you kissed me.' He watched her face as she picked up a tabloid paper and scanned the headline.

Her face was expressionless as she scanned the photograph. *Truly a time for miracles—Rio in love.* Some of the tension left her. 'Well, it seems we're off the hook for another day.'

Rio's jaw tightened. 'Evie—'

'Sorry—it's just that I'm finding this whole thing quite stressful, in case you hadn't noticed. Every morning we go through the same thing. And the worst thing is, there is never going to come a point when it goes away—they have that photo for ever, don't they? They can use it this year or next year—it never ends.'

Wondering exactly when he'd developed a conscience, Rio forced a reluctant confession past his lips. 'Evie, they won't use that photo.'

She looked up from the newspaper. 'It's all very well to say that while you're giving them something more interesting to print, but sooner or later they're going to get bored with our "romance" and then they'll be on the lookout for something more juicy.'

'I can guarantee they're not going to print that photograph.'

'How? Has your security team managed to track the man down?' With a soft gasp, she dropped the newspaper on the table. 'They found him?'

He had to tell her now. 'Yes. We found him.'

Relief crossed her face, to be followed quickly by consternation. 'But that doesn't mean you can stop the photograph. I mean, he's had loads of time to have sent it all over the place. It's probably too late.'

'He hasn't sent it anywhere. My security team confiscated his camera.'

'But how—'

'They confiscated his camera less than fifteen seconds after he took the offending photograph,' Rio confessed in a raw tone, telling himself firmly that he'd do exactly the same thing again in the same circumstances. 'That's how I know for a fact that he didn't send it anywhere. Antonio was outside the door of the Penthouse. He apprehended the guy before he'd taken two steps.'

A heavy silence descended on the room. Evie stared at him, digesting the enormity of his confession and Rio felt the tension inside himself double.

'You're saying—' she swallowed hard '—you're telling me—oh, my God.' She sank down hard on the nearest sofa, her breathing rapid. 'There was never a risk that the photo-graph would be published. You told me…you let me think…' She lifted her head to look at him and her eyes were huge and shocked. 'How could you do that?'

'Because it was necessary. It was the right thing to do.'

'The right thing?' She lifted her hands to her face and then let them drop again, clearly struggling to find the words to express herself. 'I was almost out of my *mind* with worry! My grandfather is eighty-six years old and I thought…I thought…' Her face was contorted with pain. 'I thought it would crucify him to see that photo. I was *so* worried—'

'Which is why I assured you that they wouldn't use the pictures.'

'But you didn't tell me *why* you were so sure!' She stood up, shock giving way to anger. 'You arranged the photogra-pher! You were in league with creepy Carlos!'

'No—' Rio interrupted her hastily '—that isn't true. It *was* a set-up.' He raked his fingers through his hair, wondering how, of all the difficult negotiations he'd ever made, this one seemed the most challenging. 'But I admit that I turned it to my advantage. I had no choice.'

'You *did* have a choice. There is always a choice. You could have told me the truth.'

'I didn't know if you were involved or not.'

'I *told* you I wasn't.'

He decided not to waste time pointing out that plenty of her sex lied for a living. In the short time he'd known her, he'd started to realise that Evie didn't seem to think the same way as other women. 'By the time I realised that you were telling the truth, we were already deeply involved in the pretence. I was afraid you'd walk out on me.'

'So you used me. Is that what you're trying to tell me?'

Unable to find an alternative take on the situation, Rio felt sweat prickle his brow. 'Yes.'

'But you...' She jabbed her fingers into her hair, an expression of shocked disbelief on her face. 'But we had sex—what was your justification for that? Were there cameras in the room?'

'You initiated the sex.'

She gave a painful laugh. 'Well, that's you off the hook, then.' Her eyes were glazed with tears. 'You warned me you were ruthless and you told me that I'd find it easy to dump you—well, you were right. I'm dumping you. We now have the shortest engagement on record.'

'I accept that I was wrong not to tell you,' Rio breathed, 'but *don't* walk out.'

'Why? Because you haven't closed your precious deal yet? What is *wrong* with you? You don't need more money but you're so desperate to win you're willing to do whatever it takes.' A toss of her head sent her hair flaming down her back and she stalked back into the bedroom without glancing in his direction, flinging words over her shoulder like missiles. 'There are some things in life that are more important than money, Rio. People's feelings are more important. Integrity. Honesty. And if you don't know what any of those words mean then use some of that money of yours to buy a dictionary.'

Rio searched his brain for slick words that would extricate him from this hole, but found none. His instinct was to leave her alone, but his legs had different ideas and, moments later, he found himself standing in the doorway of the bedroom, watching her.

'I understood that you were worried, which is why I

constantly reassured you that the photograph would not be published. You should have trusted me.'

'Trusted you!' She turned on him, her eyes flashing. 'Why would I trust you? You're impossibly arrogant. You think you're right about everything. How was I to know that in this case the reason you knew the photograph wouldn't be published was because you had it in your possession all the time? I don't believe this is happening—' Her breathing was shallow and rapid. 'You were so angry with Carlos. I thought you were going to finish him off—but why would he have arranged that photograph?'

'Because Carlos is the brother of a woman I once had a relationship with,' Rio said savagely. 'It was a difficult relationship. She wanted more—'

'Then she was looking in the wrong place, wasn't she?' Her tone acid, Evie scraped her make-up from the top of the dressing table into her bag. 'Didn't she read the newspapers? Didn't she know that you don't do "more"?'

Telling himself that her anger was only to be expected, Rio ploughed ahead. 'She wanted me to marry her.'

'She wanted to spend the rest of her life with you? Clearly she was deranged.'

Knowing that he deserved that, Rio took it on the chin. 'She stopped taking contraception.'

Evie paused, a tube of lipgloss in her hand. 'She became pregnant? On purpose?' The shock in her voice almost made him smile.

'Yes, on purpose. On purpose, Evie.' He said the word twice, each time with emphasis, knowing that she had absolutely no idea what people could be like. She was such a crazy idealist, wasn't she? 'Are you going to ask me why?'

'I'm not stupid. I presume she thought you'd marry her.' She stuffed the lipgloss into her bag. 'Which, of course, you wouldn't.'

'No, because it never would have worked.' Rio growled

the words angrily. 'I offered her everything but that. I offered to buy her a house near me—I offered her financial support. But all she wanted was marriage and I'd made the mistake of being honest about how much I wanted to see my child. She used that knowledge to carry on blackmailing me. Only this time, instead of "I'm pregnant, marry me", it was "if you want to see your child, marry me".'

Evie stood still. Some of the anger in her face was replaced by uncertainty.

'She used my child as currency,' Rio said thickly. 'An object to be bartered with. I gave her sufficient funds to live in luxury for the rest of her life but she frittered it away on unsuitable friends and people I would not have allowed anywhere near my daughter. Because she had my child, I carried on trying to help. I even gave her useless brother Carlos a job in my hotel, under close supervision. But I was working behind the scenes to get custody of my daughter.'

'Custody?' Her eyes widened in shock and he gave a bitter smile because he'd seen exactly that same look on the faces of others.

'Yes, custody. And, yes, I know I'm a single man. A single man with a self-confessed relationship phobia. I am no one's image of ideal father material. It was easy for her to build a case, making me look unsuitable. I work inhuman hours, I have no history of commitment—' he breathed deeply '—it's possible I would never even have had a chance if it weren't for the fact that Jeanette left Elyssa unattended.'

'She left her child *alone*?'

Rio wanted to tell her not to be so naive, but realised that would be unfair. It wasn't naivety that prevented her from understanding why another woman might leave a child alone; it was her nature. He'd seen the way she cared about her grandfather. She was warm and loving—a nurturer who believed that families stuck together and supported each other through thick and thin.

'Jeanette didn't ever want a child. All she wanted was a tool to manipulate me. She doesn't have a maternal bone in her body.' He watched Evie flinch as he took a hatchet to her illusions. 'I imagine someone like you would find that almost impossible to believe, so let me tell you just how unhappy my daughter's life has been so far and maybe then you'll understand that there are times when "ruthless" is justified.'

'Rio—'

'She was left on her own in the house because there was no way Jeanette was wasting any of the money I gave her caring for a child she never wanted. I sent her staff; she fired them. I interviewed eight nannies personally. None of them lasted a day. Jeanette said she'd care for Elyssa herself, but she didn't. I've been fighting for custody since before my daughter was born but it was only six months ago, after she had a nasty fall in the house while she was on her own, that the tide turned in my favour. The police were called. Elyssa was taken into foster care while they reviewed the case. It's been a long, hard slog but we were almost there.'

'Were?'

'Elyssa is Jeanette's meal ticket,' Rio said, struggling to keep the emotion out of his voice. 'She doesn't want me to have custody. She reinvented herself as a model mother. She's been volunteering at the church, visiting the sick and the elderly, generally behaving like a perfect citizen.'

'And at the same time she's been trying to destroy your reputation? Make you look like an unsuitable carer for a child?'

'Unfortunately, over the years, I've managed to do that for myself. I've made no apology for the fact that I don't want commitment, never realising that the time would come when I'd regret expressing those sentiments in such a public fashion.'

'So that's why Carlos wanted me to spend the night. That's why he arranged the photographer. That's what the deal is.'

Her breathing quickened and her eyes held his. 'This deal isn't about money, is it? It isn't business. It's your daughter. The reason you didn't want those photographs published was because of your daughter. They were trying to make you look bad.'

Rio stood still, watching her. So much was riding on this conversation and yet, for once, his slick way with words had abandoned him. 'I've worked for years to reach this point.'

'But if your security team caught the man immediately—if you knew there was no danger of that photograph being exposed—why go through with that farce?'

'Because I thought you could help my case.' He didn't flinch from the truth. 'My lawyer told me to stay whiter than white or find a wholesome-looking woman. Until Carlos intervened, I'd settled on the first option. Then I saw you lying on the bed.'

'I was naked,' she said dryly. 'Not exactly wholesome.'

'No one looking at you could ever believe you were anything other than a thoroughly decent person,' Rio said roughly. *And he'd used her.* 'I'm a man who has said I'd never settle down—to convince people I'd changed my mind, it would have to be with someone completely different from the usual women I date. You fitted that description.'

She stood for a moment. 'And it didn't occur to you to just tell me the truth? You could have just asked for my help. You could have trusted me.'

'No, I couldn't.'

'Have you ever trusted a woman?'

Rio didn't even hesitate. 'I've never had reason to.'

Pain flickered across her face and he knew she was thinking about everything they'd shared. 'So what happens now?'

He clenched his fists by his sides, wondering why it suddenly felt so hard to remain detached when that was his normal default mode. 'That's your decision,' he said flatly.

'If you want to go home to your grandfather for Christmas, then I can arrange that. And of course you have a job as receptionist. You're overqualified for the position, but if that's what you want then that's fine by me. The one thing I ask is that you dump me, as we agreed, rather than telling the media the truth.'

'How have you kept your daughter's name out of the press?'

'That was part of my deal with Jeanette. And I admit we've been lucky. I suppose because I'm the last man in the world to want a child, they didn't look.'

'So you want me to dump you—' She rubbed her fingers across her forehead. 'But you haven't won your case yet, have you? I could make things difficult for you.'

'Yes.' The thought brought a bitter taste to his mouth. 'But I'll have to take that chance.'

'What makes you think you're the right home for a little girl, Rio? What can you offer a child?'

He didn't hesitate. 'Security. The absolute certainty that I'll always be there for her.' He'd never felt the need to explain or defend his decision to anyone before, but suddenly he had a burning need to defend himself to Evie. 'I'm not planning to nominate myself for super-dad any time soon, but I can offer her a stability that has never been present in her life.'

'That's quite a promise, coming from a man who doesn't believe in commitment.'

'This is one commitment I'm prepared to make.' He didn't expect her to believe him. How could he when he was well aware he'd given her no reason on which to base that belief?

And already his mind was computing the options because he knew she was going to walk out. Why wouldn't she? He'd deceived her. He'd used her. He'd hurt her. *He'd had sex with her—*

And now she was going to make him pay.

He needed to ring the lawyers and warn them, although what they would be able to do, he had no idea.

Reaching into his pocket for his phone, his fingers encountered his wallet. He paused and then pulled it out and retrieved the photograph from behind a stack of dollars. Hesitating for only a fraction of a second, he handed it to her. 'This is Elyssa. It's not a brilliant one—I took it with my phone in the summer. Her hair is darker than it looks in the photograph.' He watched as she stared down at the photograph.

'Please leave me alone,' she said hoarsely. 'I need a minute to myself.'

Rio hesitated, and then turned and walked back into the living room. Conscious of how much he'd hurt her, he retrieved his BlackBerry from his jacket pocket. The only option open to him now was damage limitation.

He was in the process of dialling his lawyer when her voice came from behind him.

'Put the phone down.' She stood in the doorway, stiff and unsmiling, the photograph still in her hand. 'I'll stay and finish this charade if you think it will help you. Not because you shoved a photograph of a vulnerable little girl into my hand and made me feel guilty which, by the way, was yet another example of ruthless manipulation on your part, but because you took that photograph in the first place. It's the first time I've ever known you to use your BlackBerry for anything other than work. If you carry a picture of your daughter around, there must be some good in you somewhere. I have yet to see it, but I live in hope. Unlike you, I'm prepared to take some things on trust. Given that Elyssa seems to have drawn the short straw with her mother, she needs someone who is prepared to stand up and fight for her, *not* that I think that excuses your appalling behaviour.'

Stunned by her words, Rio inhaled deeply. 'Evie—'

'And you need to learn to take some things on trust, too.

You need to show some faith in people.' She walked across the room and placed the photograph carefully in his hand. 'A little girl's future is at stake—you should have known I'd do the right thing. I didn't need a guilt trip to set me on the right path. If you'd told me the truth in the first place—' there were tears in her eyes '—I just wish you had told me the truth, Rio.'

'My daughter's future was all that mattered to me.'

'If you'd told me, I would have helped you.' Her lashes sparkled with moisture. 'You need to stop being such a cynic because the last thing a little girl needs is a father who is a cynic. When you're reading her fairy stories, maybe it's right to adapt the ending—maybe it isn't right to tell children that they all lived happily ever after, I don't know—but neither is it right to bring her up believing that everyone is guilty until proven innocent. That there is no good in anyone. That all people are out to get what they can out of everyone else. If you're going to apply corporate principles to parenting, then it's never going to work.' Taking a deep breath, she squared her shoulders. 'Now, get your coat and phone that driver of yours. We're going shopping.'

Still braced for catastrophe, it took Rio a few moments to assimilate the fact that she wasn't leaving. She was offering to stay. Her generosity floored him. 'Of course I'll take you shopping.' His voice was husky with an emotion he didn't recognise and he lifted his hand and brushed a strand of hair away from her moist cheek. Gratitude, he thought. And admiration. He realised that he'd been wrong about her again. She was far, far stronger than she looked. 'I'll buy you the biggest diamond you've ever seen as long as you tell me I'm forgiven.'

'I didn't say anything about diamonds and I didn't say anything about forgiveness. We're going to a toy shop. If you truly intend to be a father to Elyssa, then you need to start learning what little girls like for Christmas.' Despite everything, there was humour in her gaze. 'I probably ought to warn you that I'm something of an expert. Fasten your seat belt because I have a feeling this is going to be a steep learning curve.'

CHAPTER EIGHT

'FAIRY wings?' RIO's tone was incredulous. 'You're sure?'

Evie reached for a pair of pink gossamer wings which hung from a metal hook. She felt devastated. Ripped to shreds by the revelation that he'd lied to her. 'Trust me, fairy wings are always a hit with four-year-olds. Better buy a spare pair, ready for when she breaks these.' It felt strange, having this conversation with this man. She had a sense that what she was saying was as alien to him as the Russian Vladimir spoke.

As if to confirm her suspicions, he looked at her blankly. 'Why will she break them? She's a little girl, not a Sumo wrestler—'

'Yes, but she'll want to sleep in them,' Evie explained patiently, 'because that's what little girls always do and sleeping in them will break them. When that happens you can either explain to her that they're gone for ever or you can spoil her rotten and get her another pair. Normally I'd suggest it's dangerous to spoil her but, given that she's obviously had a completely rubbish time lately, I think an extra pair is probably in order.'

Without hesitation, Rio cleared the shelves of pink fairy wings.

'I meant one spare pair,' Evie said faintly, 'not ten.'

'I'm not risking anything. As you say, she's had enough trauma for one lifetime.' Rio handed them to his stunned bodyguard. 'So we have fairy wings and spare fairy wings and spare spare fairy wings. What next?'

Thrown by the sight of the normally taciturn Antonio struggling to balance a mountain of fairy wings, Evie managed a smile. 'If you're attacked now, this will be interesting. You'll just have to bash them with your magic wand or something—'

Antonio's mouth twitched. 'I'll remember that.'

'Don't worry about Antonio,' Rio drawled. 'He probably trained in the same unarmed combat camp as your grandfather. If the chips were down, he'd find a way to turn fairy wings into an assault weapon.' His gaze met hers. 'It's good of you to do this for me.'

She felt frozen inside. 'I'm doing it for her, not you.' She ignored the tiny part of her that questioned that claim, just as she ignored the commotion in her nerve-endings that told her he was even more lethally attractive when he was vulnerable. 'Let's go. We need dolls.'

'I'm not sure about dolls. Last time I saw her, I took her a doll.' He scanned the rows of toys with something close to despair. 'I think I probably chose the wrong sort. There were millions. The one I picked had a very elaborate costume and she was very frustrated when it wouldn't come off.'

Evie's heart twisted at that image—the arrogant, self assured tycoon taking a serious knock to his self-esteem as he struggled to choose a doll. 'I expect she'd like a doll that can be dressed and undressed. They make one that cries and wets itself.'

His expression was comical. 'There is a market for that?'

'A huge market,' Evie told him, enjoying the look of shock on his face. 'You pour the milk in one end and it comes out the other, just like real life.'

Rio shuddered and he said something in Italian. 'That is *fun*?'

'It's role play. Didn't you ever play mummies and daddies—?' Evie took one look at his face and shook her head. 'Forget I said that. I don't suppose commitment games were ever your thing. Take it from me, most little girls are a sucker for caring for a baby. Put a real baby in a room and the girls are all over it in minutes. Whatever anyone says about feminism, most little girls love pretending dolls are babies.'

'Did you?' Suddenly his gaze became disturbingly acute and Evie felt the slow burn of colour in her cheeks.

'Yes.' She turned away from him and took the stairs two at a time. There were some things it didn't pay to think about. Especially not around this man. She just wanted to get this over with so that she could go into hiding and lick her wounds. 'Here—dolls. I'll grab a shopping trolley. I don't think poor Antonio can carry any more.'

'A whole floor of dolls?' Rio looked horrified. 'How do you know where to start?'

Evie tried to translate it into terms he'd understand. 'Like any product, you have to segment your market. There's a specific market for young children. Then they segment the market again—dolls that cry, dolls that—'

'OK, fine. I get the picture—' he interrupted her hastily '—so which is the market leader?'

'This one.' She pointed and Rio lifted it off the shelf gingerly.

'How many spares do we need?'

'At least one. It's very easy to leave a doll on a plane.' Suddenly realising what she'd said, Evie gave a wry smile. 'On the other hand, you do *own* the plane, so you'd be able to retrieve it without long and fruitless arguments with unhelpful airline staff. You could probably get away without spares.'

Clearly not prepared to take any risks, Rio added five identical dolls to the growing pile of toys in the trolley. 'I have five homes,' he said by way of explanation. 'It's probably best to have a spare in each.'

'Five?' Evie blinked. 'You have *five* homes?'

'You're thinking that it will confuse a small child?' He added a small stack of accessories to the pile. 'I've been thinking the same thing. In fact, I've been restructuring my business so that I can spend as much time as possible at my palazzo in Florence, to give her stability. My team have decorated a room exactly like the one she is in at the moment so that it seems familiar. It's right next to mine and I have already appointed a very experienced English nanny who is ready to move in at a moment's notice.'

Evie felt the hot sting of tears scald her eyes and turned away in horror, blinking rapidly. For crying out loud, what was the matter with her? Why did the thought of him studying a child's room and creating an identical version make her want to sob? Struggling for control, she picked up a doll from the shelf and pretended to examine it. Her insides were at war and, when she felt Rio's hand close over her shoulder, the tears formed a lump in her throat. 'This is a good one.' She thrust the doll at him and he studied it in silence.

'Are you sure? I'm no expert, but I don't think so.'

Dragging her gaze from the dark shadow of his jaw to the doll she'd handed him, Evie realised that he was right. The doll she'd selected was completely unsuitable for a young child. Apart from the fact that the clothing was covered in intricate beading, there was a clear warning that it wasn't intended for children under the age of eight. She wasn't concentrating. Her mind was all over the place.

His hand still on her shoulder, Rio returned the doll to the shelf. 'I've upset you again.' His voice was low and all Evie could do was shake her head, frightened by the intensity of her feelings.

'No.'

'You're trying not to cry. I know enough about women to recognise the signs.'

'I believe you. I'm sure you've made enough women cry in your time.'

'But normally they don't try and hold it back. As usual, you have to be different. If you want to sob, then sob. I know I deserve it. I really have been a bastard to you.' He smoothed her hair away from her face but she moved her head away sharply.

'Don't touch me. And don't use that word in a toy shop.' Evie almost wished she could cry. It would have been easier to hate him. The problem was, she didn't hate him. She didn't hate him at all. He'd used her, he'd lied to her, but she still didn't hate him.

Ignoring her warning not to touch, he closed his hands over her shoulders. 'Evie—'

'Let's just get this done. I'm tired. I haven't had much sleep in the last few days.' She tried to pull away from him but he held her, his physical strength evident in his firm grip.

'We were talking about where Elyssa would enjoy living most. Do you have an opinion on where a little girl would like to live? I assumed a child would rather live in one place as much as possible and Florence is a wonderful city, but if you think—'

'I honestly don't know.' Evie finally managed to pull away from him. 'Why would I know? I'm not a mother. I probably know less than you do.' All she knew was that her mind was a mess. She'd told herself that he was totally the wrong man for her because he wasn't the family sort. He'd emphasised that he wasn't interested in commitment. And now she discovered he had a daughter he clearly adored and every decision he made, even the one to use her so ruthlessly to achieve his own ends, demonstrated the level of his commitment to his child. The fact that he was clearly struggling so hard to do the right thing somehow made the whole thing all the more poignant. He hadn't chosen fatherhood, but he was determined to do it right. He was facing his responsibilities. Despite what everyone said, Rio Zaccarelli didn't have a problem with commitment. His problem was with his own relationships with women. And that was hardly surprising, was it, given the women he'd met in the past?

Thinking about Elyssa's mother, Evie's throat was thick with emotion. Who would do that to a man? Or to a child? A solid lump seemed to have formed behind the wall of her chest. She kept seeing him removing that photograph from his wallet. Kept seeing him piling up fairy wings so that his daughter didn't suffer any more trauma. Her arm brushed against his and an electric current shot through her body and, at that moment, the truth lit up in her brain.

She'd fallen in love with him. At some point during the glittering, glamorous charade, the pretence had turned to reality.

It was a thrilling, sickening feeling. A sudden whoosh of the heart and a sinking of the stomach. Dread and desire intermingled with a knowledge that the whole thing was hopeless.

How could that have happened?

In such a short time and with a man like him?

How could she have been so recklessly foolish?

Parading his faults through her brain, Evie turned sharply and walked towards the end of the store, hiding her panic. 'You need books. Reading together is a great way to bond.' She blocked out an image of Rio sprawled on a bedcover covered in pink dancing fairies, reading to a small, dark haired girl who adored him. This was hard enough without making it worse for herself.

Her hands shook as she selected books from the shelves, conscious of his steady scrutiny.

'What's going on, Evie? When we came into this store you were hell bent on punishing me—you dragged me round pink fairy wings, handed me dolls and stuffed toys bigger than I am—and suddenly you look like the one who is being punished. You look like someone who has had a terrible shock.'

'No,' she answered quickly. Too quickly. 'Not a shock.'

'I wish you'd tell me why you're upset. Or is this still because you're thinking about my daughter?' He sat down on a chair in the reading area. He should have looked ridiculous, stretching his powerful body and long legs amongst the small bean bags and tiny colouring tables, but he didn't look ridiculous. Evie doubted Rio could look ridiculous anywhere. He had that ability to blend with his surroundings that came with confidence and self-assurance.

'Of course I'm thinking of your daughter.' Picking another two books from the shelf, she flicked through them. 'That's what we're doing here, isn't it?' She wished he'd stop looking at her. Suddenly, she was afraid that everything she was feeling might show on her face. The feelings growing inside her were so new she hadn't got used to hiding them yet.

'So we've done fairy wings, dolls, stuffed toys, games—' he listed them one by one, a trace of irony in his voice '—is there anything else you think she would like? What does a little girl really want?'

What does a little girl really want?

Evie stared for a moment, the question opening a deep rift inside her. It was the one thing she was able to answer with complete confidence. 'All a little girl really wants is her daddy,' she said huskily. 'The rest is just icing on the cake.'

'You're sure?' Rio tucked the phone between his ear and his shoulder as he opened the email. 'Yes, I have it here…I'm reading it right now…I'll make all the arrangements.'

When he finally ended the call, he knew his life had altered irrevocably. It was done. The lawyers had finally confirmed it. Elyssa was going to come and live with him. The courts had awarded him custody.

His gaze slid to the small mountain of toys that had been neatly stacked in one corner of the Penthouse, a testament to Evie's dedication to her task. His little girl would want for nothing, not that he was kidding himself for one moment that the future was going to go as smoothly as that one shopping trip. For a start there was his own inexperience to take into account, and then there was the inescapable fact that Elyssa had spent the past few years with a woman so self-absorbed that the needs of her child had largely gone unnoticed. Whichever way you looked at it, there was a rocky road ahead. Staring at the toys, he suddenly wished Evie was there to guide him through more than just his choice of doll.

But that was a crazy thought, wasn't it? A selfish thought, because he had nothing to offer her. Not even a defence against her accusation that he'd used her.

He had.

He'd done what needed to be done, without a flicker of conscience. But he didn't need to use her a moment longer. Their charade could end. Evie could get on with her life— could concentrate on making her grandfather proud.

She could go home for Christmas.

He sat there for a long moment and for once his phones were silent.

Through the wraparound glass of the luxurious Penthouse, he could see that the snow was falling again and immediately he thought how pleased Evie would be.

She loved snow.

Rising to his feet, he decided he needed to tell her, but when he searched the Penthouse there was no sign of her. At some point during his endless phone calls, she'd gone out.

Antonio entered the suite in response to his urgent call. 'Miss Anderson has gone to the park, boss.'

'What do you mean, she's gone to the park? It's seven

degrees below freezing and it's still snowing—' Rio prowled across the thick carpet. The snow was floating past the window, thick flakes that landed on the ground and settled. The streets were virtually empty of people and traffic, everyone trapped indoors because of the weather. For the first time in over a decade the pond in the park had frozen over. A few ducks waddled sorrowfully across the ice. Staring through the window, he peered through the swirling flakes but failed to spot her. 'What the hell is she doing in the park?'

Antonio cleared his throat. 'She's building a snowman, boss.'

'She's—*what?*'

'A snowman.' Antonio was smiling. 'It's surprisingly good, actually. She's managed to—'

'Spare me a description of the snowman.' Rio spoke through his teeth. 'Did she leave a message for me?'

'Yes. She said to tell you that she needed fresh air and that she'd be back when she was finished.'

'Where exactly is she?'

'The far side of the pond, sir. Shall I call your driver?'

Rio strode across the room and snatched his coat from the back of the chair. 'No. I'll walk.'

'In that case, perhaps you would give this to Evie, sir, with my compliments.' Antonio dug his hand in his pocket and withdrew a carrot. 'I went down to the kitchens and found it for her. She might find it useful.'

Rio stared at it. 'Call me stupid,' he said slowly, 'but I can't for a moment imagine what possible use she will have for a single raw carrot.'

'Then you've obviously never made a snowman, boss. It's for his nose. I tried to get a slightly smaller one, but the kitchen—'

'All right—I get the picture.' Feeling out of touch with everyone around him, Rio pushed the carrot into his pocket and strode across the room to the private elevator. As he reached the doors, he paused, his mind exploring an idea. His instinct was to reject it instantly, but for once he fought that instinct.

Why not?

It would please her and he certainly owed her a small bite of happiness after the way he'd treated her.

Having delivered his instructions to a bemused Antonio, Rio left the hotel and crossed the snowy street, wondering what on earth he was doing chasing a girl across a park in the freezing cold.

He found her kneeling in the snow, scooping snow into balls and adding them to a snowman, who was now wearing her hat. Her hair spilled over the shoulders of her quilted jacket and her cheeks were pink from the cold. Her lips were moving and at first he thought she was talking to herself, and then he realised that she was singing.

'Five gold rings, four calling birds, three French hens—'

'—and a girl with double pneumonia,' Rio drawled as he walked over to her. He pulled the carrot out of his pocket and handed it to her. 'Here. Give the guy a nose so that you can come inside and warm up.'

'I'm fine. I'm happy here. Thanks for the carrot.' Without looking at him, she pressed it into the snowman's face and sat back on her heels. 'What do you think?'

Rio decided that this was probably one of those occasions when honesty was not required. 'Spectacular,' he said tactfully. 'A real gladiator of a snowman.' Why wasn't she looking at him? He changed his position so that he could get a better look at her face and saw that her eyes were red.

He'd made her cry.

Forced to confront the damage he'd caused, Rio gave a bitter smile. The fact that she'd still been prepared to help him despite her own personal agony made him feel about as small as the snowflake that landed on his hand.

She pulled off her gloves and blew on her hands to warm them. 'There's no need to go overboard. I know you think I'm crazy.'

He thought she was astonishing. As brave as she was beautiful.

'I'm no judge of snowmen.' He dug his hands in his pockets. 'I've never seen anyone make one before. But you clearly find it an absorbing occupation so I'm willing to be converted.'

'You've never made one yourself?'

'Never.'

'Then you're missing out.' She pushed two pebbles into the snow above the carrot and then sat back to admire her handiwork.

Rio fought the sudden desire to roll her in the snow and warm her up in the most basic way known to man. 'You need to move the pebble on the left up a bit—they're not even. He's squinting.'

Flakes of snow settled on her hair as she shifted the pebble. 'What are you doing out here, Rio? Shouldn't you be on the phone, brokering some deal or sorting out a crisis?'

'I left the phones in the Penthouse.'

She managed a smile. 'All three of them? Won't the business world crumble?'

Rio suddenly discovered that he couldn't care less. 'Come back inside with me.'

The smile vanished. 'I'm happy here.'

'You're soaked through and freezing.'

'I love the snow.' Lifting her face into the falling flakes, she closed her eyes. 'If I keep my eyes shut, I'm a child again.'

Rio felt the tension flash through his body. 'And that's a good thing?'

'Oh, yes.' Clear aquamarine eyes looked into his. 'One of my favourite childhood memories is going to the forest with my grandfather to choose a tree. I used to just stand there, breathing in the smell of pine. Have you ever stood in a forest and just smelt the air? It's the most perfect smell—sharp and pungent—it gets into your nose and then your brain and suddenly you just *feel* Christmas all the way through your body. Smells do that to me. Are you the same?'

He had no idea how to answer that question. 'No,' he said finally. 'I'm not the same.'

The happiness in her eyes dimmed. 'I don't suppose you stand still long enough to notice smells. You're always on the go, pushing another deal through. You don't even take Christmas off.'

Rio looked at her, torn between wanting to know more and wanting to change the subject. 'So what did you do when you and your grandfather had chosen the tree?'

'We took it home and decorated it. That was the best part. We couldn't afford fancy decorations so Grandma and I made stars out of flour and water, baked them in the oven and painted them silver.'

Rio remembered the way she'd stared at the elaborate decorations on the Christmas tree at the ball. He found it all too easy to imagine her sitting at the kitchen table, a huge smile on her face, her hair like a burning bush. 'How long have you lived with your grandparents?'

She reached for a twig and snapped it in half. 'Since I was four years old. My parents had gone away to celebrate their wedding anniversary and I was staying with my grandparents. I remember being really excited about sleeping in their spare bedroom. It's a tiny attic room with a sloping roof and views across the lake and the forest. It felt like the biggest adventure of my life and I couldn't wait to tell my parents every last detail.' She paused and there was a sudden hitch in her breathing. 'And then my grandfather came into my room one morning and told me that they wouldn't be coming to get me. Their car hit black ice. They didn't stand a chance.'

Rio stood still, feeling hopelessly inadequate. He watched in silence as the snow fluttered onto her shoulders. Her vibrant hair was the only warmth and colour in the place. Everything was cold, including him. Her revelation deserved a response, but he had no idea what that response should be. He wasn't used to emotional confessions. People didn't confide in him. They discussed stocks and bonds, mergers and acquisitions—not feelings.

He didn't do feelings.

Wondering what had happened to all the smooth words that were always at his disposal, Rio stumbled awkwardly through foreign territory. 'So you stayed with them?'

'My grandfather had just retired. They were looking forward to enjoying some time together. They'd even booked a world cruise—' her voice was soft '—they cancelled it. They gave me a home.' She breathed deeply. 'They became my parents.'

And the love she felt for her grandfather was a living, palpable thing. He saw it in her eyes and in her smile. In everything she did.

'You're lucky.' The moment he said the words, he braced himself for a sharp comeback. She was going to tell him that he was the lucky one. She was going to remind him that he was a billionaire with five houses and a private jet.

But she didn't say any of those things. Instead, she wiped snow from her cheeks with her gloved hand and nodded. 'I know I'm lucky. That's why I was so upset and worried about that photograph of me naked. After everything they did for me—all the sacrifices they made so that I could have a warm, loving home—I couldn't bear that my grandfather would think I'd let him down like that. All I've ever wanted is to make them proud of me.' She bit her lip. 'I'm still mad with you for not putting me out of my misery sooner, but I'm also just so relieved that Antonio intercepted the guy so quickly. It could have been worse.'

Her pragmatic approach intensified his feelings of guilt and Rio swore softly under his breath. 'I was wrong to do what I did.'

'No, you weren't. You did what you needed to do for your little girl.' She rocked back on her heels and studied her snowman. 'You were prepared to do anything to protect her. I like that. It's good. It's what families should do. They should stick together, no matter what. Family should be the one dependable thing in a person's life.'

'Why is your grandfather so desperate for you to be married?'

'I've told you—he's old-fashioned.' Picking up the other half of the twig, she pushed it into the other side of the snowman. 'He believes that as long as you have family, everything can be all right with the world.'

'All right, *now* I feel seriously guilty,' Rio said gruffly and she smiled up at him, a sparkling smile that warmed the freezing air because it was delivered with such bravery.

'If you're capable of feeling guilt, then there's hope for you, Mr Zaccarelli.'

Was there? He'd lived without that emotion for so long he wasn't even sure he knew how it felt.

'Come back to the hotel. It's absolutely freezing out here.'

'Are you telling me you're cold? Big tough guy like you?' Her voice was teasing and her eyes danced with mockery as she looked up at him. 'You're a wimp. My grandfather will be relieved when I give you the boot. He wants me to find a real man, not some shivering, pathetic creature who can't stand a shift in the weather.'

She squealed with shock and laughter as Rio moved swiftly and tumbled her backwards onto the snow.

'Are you calling me a wimp?' His mouth brushed her soft lips, tasting softness and laughter. He was about to turn the kiss into something less playful when she stuffed a handful of snow down the front of his sweater. Rio swore fluently as the ice froze his skin. 'Is that your test of a real man?'

'That's just one of them. I started with something gentle. I didn't want to be too hard on you.' She was still laughing but, because he had her body trapped under his, he felt the change in her. Looking into her eyes, he saw something that sucked the humour out of the situation—something he'd seen many times before in a woman's eyes.

For a second he couldn't move and he wondered if she even realised what she'd revealed, lying there under him with her hopes and dreams exposed.

And then he sprang to his feet, his withdrawal an instinctive reaction pre-programmed by life experience and a bone-deep cynicism about the durability of relationships. It would be cruel, wouldn't it, to hurt her more than he already had—this child-woman who still believed in happy endings.

'You're shivering.' Keeping his tone matter of fact, he hauled her to her feet and brushed the snow off her jacket. She was looking past him and for a moment he thought she was just avoiding eye contact, and then he saw her expression change. 'What's the matter?'

'Behind you,' she muttered. 'Another photographer. Why are people so interested in your life? Everywhere you go there is a bigger, longer camera lens. We'd better look as though we're in love.' The word tripped off her tongue as if it had no significance and Rio stared down into her sweet, honest face, wondering whether she'd tell him the truth.

But she didn't say anything and he felt something tug inside him.

'We don't have to do that. We can end this charade whenever we like. It's over.' He slid his hands into her hair, suddenly realising he no longer had a legitimate excuse to kiss her.

'What do you mean?' Her eyes widened and then shone as she grasped the implications of his words. 'Are you saying—?

Oh, Rio—you have custody? I'm so pleased! That's fantastic.'
She flung her arms round his neck and hugged him tightly,
whooping with joy and kissing him over and over again. Her
eyes glistened with tears of joy and he brushed them away
with his thumb, fascinated by the way she showed her emotions so freely; touched that her pleasure for his daughter
could transcend her own pain.

'There is still some red tape to play with, but my lawyers
think that Elyssa will come and live with me the week after
Christmas. For what it's worth, they think that seeing me
with you tipped the balance.'

'Well, I'm glad about that. So what does this mean?'

What did it mean? Rio had been searching for the answer
to that question.

When women had fallen in love with him before he'd
always considered it to be a question of 'buyer beware'. They
should have known better.

But Evie lived her life by a different rule book.

'Let's go back to the hotel. I have a surprise for you.'

It was over.

She no longer had a part to play in creating this happy
family.

Evie stood in the elevator, trying to keep the smile on her
face. It was selfish of her, wasn't it, to feel so devastated? The
whole reason this charade could now end was that someone
extremely sensible had decided that a little girl should live
with her daddy. As someone who had known that terrifying
feeling of loneliness and abandonment, she should be thrilled
that another little girl's dreams were going to come true. And
she was. She really was. But was she a wicked person to wish
that she could have had just a couple more days?

Forcing her own feelings aside, she smiled at Rio, determined not to make a fool of herself. *She didn't want his pity.*
The only thing she wanted from him was something quite

different. Something he wasn't able to give. 'You have plans to make. Just let me know what you want me to do.' She kept her voice brisk and practical. 'How you want me to handle things.'

He frowned. 'Handle what?'

'I'm going to dump you, remember? And, boy, am I going to enjoy that part.' Evie rubbed her hands together, wondering whether her voice sounded just a little forced.

'We'll discuss details later.' There was a tension in his shoulders that she attributed to his reaction to the momentous news. Either that or his ego was struggling with the notion of being publicly rejected.

It seemed incredible to her now that only weeks earlier she'd been about to marry another man. What she'd shared with Rio had taught her that what she'd shared with Jeff had been bland and colourless, like existing on a diet of bread and water and then suddenly discovering the variety of colour and texture of real food.

She wondered if she'd ever find anyone else who made her feel the way Rio did.

Blinking rapidly, Evie reinforced her smile as the elevator doors opened. 'Building snowmen is hungry work, so I certainly hope that—' She stopped, the words dissolving in her mouth as she saw the Penthouse.

It had been transformed from an elegant living space into a sparkling winter paradise.

Silver snowflakes were twisted through boughs of holly and an enormous Christmas tree, even bigger than the one she'd decorated, took pride of place next to the fire. It looked like a child's fantasy.

The only thing missing was Santa.

The moment the thought entered her head, Santa appeared from the second bedroom, complete with red robes and full white beard.

Evie blinked. And then she peered closer, through the

clouds of ridiculous white beard, and started to laugh. 'Antonio? Is that you in there?'

'Ho, ho, ho—'

Appalled to find tears in her eyes, Evie kept smiling. 'That doesn't quite work with an Italian accent. First fairy wings, now Santa—your job description seems to have shifted slightly over the past week.'

'I have a gift for you.' Overplaying his role like mad, Antonio reached into his sack with a flourish and pulled out a large square parcel. 'This has your name on it.'

Evie took it, wondering what all this meant. 'Am I supposed to keep it until Christmas?'

'No, you open it,' Rio said immediately as he urged her further into the room, away from Antonio who discreetly let himself out of the Penthouse.

Evie looked around her, unable to believe what she saw. 'But you don't...you hate...' She swallowed. 'You've done this for your little girl. I thought Elyssa couldn't be with you for Christmas.'

'I haven't done this for Elyssa.' His voice was rough and held a touch of uncertainty. 'I've done it for you.'

'For me?'

'Because you love Christmas and, this last week, I've deprived you of Christmas. I'm making up for it. Open the present. I hope you like it.' His eyes were wary and Evie wanted to say that the only present she wanted was him, but she couldn't, could she?

He didn't want that and it took two people to make a relationship work.

Dipping her head, she ripped the paper off the box and opened it. At first she thought there was nothing inside, and then she saw the envelope.

Puzzled, she discarded all the packaging and opened it. Inside was a printed ticket and it took a moment for her to understand what it meant. As the words sank into her brain, she gasped. 'I can spend Christmas Day with my grandfather?'

'Because the snow is so bad and your roads are pathetic, I am going to fly you by helicopter to this place where your grandfather lives—' Looking ridiculously pleased with himself, Rio outlined the plan. 'We will all spend the day together.'

Looking at Rio, with his sleek, expensive clothes and his taste for the best in everything, Evie gave a disbelieving laugh. 'Rio, you eat in hideously expensive restaurants—your chefs are the best in the world—I'm sorry, but I can't see you eating Christmas lunch in the Cedar Court Retirement Home.'

'*Sì,* I have thought the same thing myself,' Rio confessed, 'which is why two of my top chefs are currently preparing to cook lunch in more challenging surroundings than usual.'

'You're kidding.'

'It will be a true test of their talents, don't you agree?'

'But who is cooking lunch in your restaurants?'

'Someone. I don't know.' He spread his hands in a gesture that was pure Italian. 'I don't micro-manage every part of my business.'

'But if they don't do a good job, they're fired.'

'Very possibly. Are you pleased with your gift?'

Evie found it hard to speak. The fact that he'd done this made everything all the more mixed up in her head. Would it have been easier if he hadn't been so thoughtful? *Would it have been easier to walk away cursing him?* 'I'm *so* pleased,' she said huskily, standing on tiptoe and kissing him. 'Thank you. Can I phone him and tell him?'

'He might be rather busy. All the residents are currently with a stylist, choosing new outfits for Christmas Day.'

Overwhelmed by his generosity, Evie swallowed. 'Rio— you didn't have to do this—'

'I wanted to. As a thank you.' He slid his hands into her hair and brought his mouth down to hers and Evie immediately responded, wrapping her arms around his strong neck and pressing her body against his.

As a thank you. Of course. What else?

And she knew it was also a goodbye.

After tomorrow, it would be over. She wouldn't see him again.

He hadn't said what he wanted to do about ending their relationship in public, but presumably he'd chosen to wait until after Christmas Day so that her grandfather wasn't upset.

Rio pressed his mouth to her neck and gave a groan. 'We probably shouldn't be doing this—'

'I want to.' Evie spoke without hesitation, her eyes closing as he slowly unzipped her coat and trailed his mouth lower. 'I want to spend tonight with you.' If this was their last night together, then she wanted something she could remember for ever. She wanted memories to keep her warm.

She couldn't have him for ever, but she could have him for now.

'You're sure?' His voice was deep and husky and she nodded.

'Completely sure.'

It was only later, much later, when she was lying in the darkness, cocooned in his arms and sleepy from his loving, that she asked the question that had been hovering on her lips for days. 'Will you tell me why you hate Christmas? You don't have to if you don't want to, but—'

'It was never a good time of year for me.' He tightened his grip on her. 'Every Christmas was a nightmare. I'm the product of a long-term affair between my mother and a very senior politician who was married with his own family. Christmas Day was the one day he always spent with them. I was eight years old when he finally found the courage to tell her he was never going to leave his wife. I found her body lying under the Christmas tree when I got up in the morning.' He spoke the words in a flat monotone, the same voice he might have used when discussing the share price.

Evie lay immobile, shock seeping through her in icy rivulets, like melting snow. The vision played out in her brain in glorious Technicolor. An excited eight-year-old dashing downstairs to see if Santa had left presents under the tree and discovering death in all its brutal glory.

She wanted to say something—she wanted to find the perfect words that would soothe and heal—but she knew that such words didn't exist. She knew from experience that there weren't always words that could smooth the horrors of life, but she also knew that human comfort could sometimes warm when the temperature of life turned bitter cold. So she tightened her grip on him and pressed her lips against his warm skin, her muffled words intended to comfort, not cure.

'The doctor had given her tablets for depression.' Now that he'd started speaking, he seemed to want to continue. 'She'd swallowed them all, along with a bottle of champagne her lover had given her for Christmas. I called an ambulance but it was too late.'

Evie's eyes filled with tears. 'So what did you do? Where did you go?' She thought of her own loving grandparents and the tears streamed down her face and dampened his skin. 'Did you have family?'

'I gave the hospital the number of my father—' he wiped her tears with his fingers and gave a humourless laugh '—that must have been quite a Christmas lunch, don't you think? I believe it was his wife who answered the phone so he probably had some explaining to do.'

'Did he take you into his family?'

'Yes, on the surface. As a senior politician he had to be

seen to be doing the right thing and I was effectively an orphan. In practice, they sent me to boarding school and tried to pretend I didn't exist. His wife saw me as a reminder of her husband's lengthy infidelity, his daughter saw me as competition and my father saw me as nothing but a bomb ready to explode his career. He told me I'd never make anything of myself.'

'He should have been ashamed of himself—'

'His career disintegrated soon after that, so I don't think life was easy for him.'

Evie pressed her damp cheek against his chest. 'So now I understand why you were prepared to fight so hard for your little girl. Why you wanted to be a father to her.' And she understood why every Christmas tree slashed at the wound he'd buried so deep. And yet he'd put his own feelings aside in order to decorate the Penthouse for her. She wanted to ask why he'd done that—*why he'd put himself through that.* 'I love you, Rio.' Suddenly it seemed terribly important that she tell him, no matter what happened when the sun rose. No matter what he thought of her. 'I love you. I know you don't love me back—I can understand why you're so afraid to love after what you learned about relationships as a child, but that doesn't change the way I feel about you. I want you to know you're loved.'

He gave a low groan and pulled her onto him, wrapping his arms around her. 'I know you love me. I saw it in your eyes when you looked at me in the park.'

'Oh.' Embarrassed, she gave a tiny laugh. 'So much for hiding my feelings. Just don't ever invite me to play poker.'

'Evie—'

'Don't say anything.' She pressed her mouth to his. 'This has happened to you a load of times before. I know it has. It's fine. Don't let's think about tomorrow. Let's just enjoy right now. Right now is all that matters.'

She lay awake in the darkness, holding him, wishing she could hold the moment for ever and stop dawn breaking.

It was the end, she knew that.

For the first time in her life, she didn't want Christmas Day to come.

CHAPTER NINE

RIO was up with the dawn, all dark shadows of the night thrown off as he showered and changed and spoke into two of his three phones while making the arrangements for the day.

Moving more slowly, Evie dressed and collected together the presents she'd bought for her grandfather. A soft cashmere scarf for his walks in the gardens of the home, a reading lamp and some of his favourite chocolates.

As Rio made the final preparations, she wandered back into the sitting room and stared wistfully at the decorations. How much courage had it taken, she thought, to adorn the Penthouse with the flavour of Christmas when the taste must be so bitter to him. A great deal of courage. Obviously, he wasn't a wimp.

He was a real man.

'Are you ready?' He strode up to her and relieved her of the parcels and Evie took a breath.

No, she wasn't ready. But she was never going to be ready for him to walk out of her life.

'I've never been on a helicopter before,' she said brightly. 'Life with you has been one big new experience.'

He smiled and kissed her on the mouth with erotic purpose. 'We're not finished yet.'

No. They had today. One whole day.

Her heart skittered and jumped and she wanted to ask him what his plans were for the announcement, but he was already striding into the elevator, this time going up to the roof, to the helicopter pad.

And then they were flying across the snow-covered English countryside and Evie thought she'd never seen anything more beautiful in her life. Beautiful and poignant because the enforced silence made her mind focus on the fact that everything she did with him today would be for the last time.

By the time they finally landed in the gardens of the Cedar Court Retirement Home, she was barely holding herself together. Even the prospect of seeing her beloved grandfather couldn't lift her sagging spirits. What made the whole thing even harder was that Rio seemed completely energized.

'I am looking forward to finally meeting your grandfather, having spoken to him so many times on the phone.'

So many times? Evie frowned. She knew he'd called her grandfather twice, but she wasn't aware of any other occasions. Before she could question him, the doors opened and she saw all the residents lined up in their finery. She saw Mrs Fitzwilliam with her hair newly styled and then there was her grandfather, dressed in his best suit and smiling proudly at the head of the line.

Within a second she was in his arms and kissing him, her tears mingling with his as they hugged and talked at the same time and he felt solid and safe and such an important part of her life that she wondered why on earth she'd ever thought she could live happily in London. Maybe she'd be all right, Evie thought as she closed her eyes and hugged him. Maybe she'd survive.

They spent precious minutes catching up and it was a few moments before she realised that the entire retirement home had been transformed into a silver and white paradise, just like the Penthouse.

'Your Rio has done us proud, that's for sure. You found

yourself a real man, Evie. I can see how much you love him,' her grandfather said gruffly and Evie's control almost cracked as she wondered how on earth she was going to explain to him when the time came to break it off. She cast a helpless glance at Rio but he merely smiled and turned to say something in Italian to Antonio.

Rio's chefs had surpassed themselves but Evie barely touched her lunch, relieved when her grandfather finally rose to make a speech and she could give up the pretence of eating. He thanked the chefs, the styling team and most of all Rio. And then he looked at Evie, his eyes full of love.

'Sometimes,' he said quietly, 'life doesn't turn out the way you plan it. When Evie came into our lives, we became parents all over again and those years were the happiest I've known. Evie, I want you to know that, no matter what happens, I'll always be proud of you. Not because of what you do, but because of who you are.'

His words cut the final thread on her control. Evie felt tears scald her eyes and she had the most awful feeling that her grandfather knew that her life had tumbled apart in London. Had he somehow discovered that she'd lost her flat and her job? Had he guessed that this whole thing with Rio was a farce? She took a gulp of the champagne Rio had provided, blinking rapidly to stop the tears from falling. She was so choked that she was relieved when Rio stood up.

And then she saw the serious look on his handsome face and relief turned to alarm. Oh, no. Please don't let him decide that this was a good time to tell the truth. Not on Christmas Day.

She wanted her grandfather to have the very best day of his life—

Her anxious gaze met Rio's and she mouthed the word *don't!* but he simply smiled as he lifted his glass.

'I agree with every word that has been spoken. Life certainly doesn't turn out the way you plan.' His voice was smooth and confident and it was clear from the way he spoke and stood that he was comfortable addressing large groups of people. 'When I arrived in London twelve days ago, my plan was to sort out a complicated business issue and then spend the next few days blocking out the fact that it's Christmas, because that's what I do. Every year I try and forget it's Christmas.' A shocked silence greeted his words and Evie felt her mouth dry as she anticipated what he might say next.

'But this year—' he paused and a faint smile touched his hard mouth '—this year I met Evie and all my plans changed. Instead of doing deals, I was dancing. Instead of analyzing shares, I was building snowmen. When I arrived in London I had no plans to fall in love and certainly no plans to get married—' he let the words hang in the air and a stunned silence spread across the room '—but that's because I didn't know that people like Evie existed.'

Nobody moved.

Evie felt as though she was going to pass out. She saw her grandfather beaming at her and several of the elderly women fanning themselves as they watched Rio standing there, tall and impossibly handsome. She felt a burst of hope, followed by a cascade of incredible joy, immediately tempered by caution because she was so terribly afraid she might have misunderstood.

Was this still pretending? Had he decided to take their charade one step further before shattering it for ever?

She glanced around, wondering if the press had some-how gained access to this private event, thinking that only a long lens could have triggered that speech from him. But there were no fancy cameras. There were no journalists or paparazzi scrambling to record the moment.

So why was he saying these things?

'Evie—' He took her hand in his and drew her firmly to

her feet. 'I know how much you love me. What you don't know is how much I love you.'

Her knees felt weak and her body started to tremble. 'Rio—'

'It's real.' Reading her mind, he pressed his mouth to hers, his kiss a lingering promise of a lifetime of love. 'This isn't for the press, or for your grandfather. It's just for us. I want you to marry me.'

'But—'

'I live and work in such a hard, cynical world. I deal with hard, cynical people—and then I met you.' He stroked her hair away from her face, watching her expression as if he were trying to interpret every blink. 'Yesterday, when I finally heard that I had what I wanted, I couldn't work out why I didn't feel more elated. And I realised it was because gaining my daughter meant losing you and I didn't want it to be that way. I'm afraid that my biggest fault is that I want everything.'

Evie was laughing through her tears. 'Greedy.'

'Yes. And selfish, and ruthless—' Smiling, unapologetic, he leaned his forehead against hers. 'You already know that I'll do whatever it takes to get what I want, and I want you, for ever, so you might as well just surrender without a fight.'

For ever?

Happiness flooded through her. 'You don't have to fight.'

'Marry me,' he murmured softly. 'We need to give your grandfather a baby to bounce on his knee and in the meantime he can make a start with Elyssa. She's in desperate need of spare family. She has us, of course, but a wise person once told me that it's useful to have spares of everything so I thought it would be good to collect some more relatives for her.'

Evie buried her face in his neck, half laughing, half crying, thinking that if this was how love felt then from now on every day was going feel like Christmas. 'I—'

'I think the rest of this conversation should be conducted in private,' Rio breathed, sweeping her into his arms so that the toe of her shoe narrowly missed the Christmas pudding. 'Please enjoy the rest of your meal. This afternoon we have dancing. And singing. And Evie will be back to give a private performance of her much acclaimed version of *The Twelve Days of Christmas* but, as that requires dancing on the tables, it has to be after we've finished eating.'

'Rio, you can't just—' Mortified, Evie turned scarlet. 'They're all looking! What do you think you're doing?'

'What am I doing?' There was laughter in his voice. 'I'm behaving like a real man, *tesoro*. If you have any complaints about that, you can take it up with your grandfather.'

Twelve months later

'Can I hold her?'

'Of course you can,' Evie said immediately. 'She's your baby sister.'

Elyssa stepped closer and peered at the baby's face. 'She's very small.'

'Well, she's only three weeks old. You were this small once.'

'But I didn't live with you then.'

'No.' Evie reached out a hand and stroked Elyssa's dark hair. 'But you live with us now. We're a family. Always.'

'I liked being your bridesmaid. I'm pleased you married my Daddy.'

Evie swallowed. 'I'm pleased, too. Now, sit back in the chair and then I'll hand Lara to you. She needs to feel secure.'

The little girl wriggled to the back of the chair and held

out her arms and Evie sat down next to her and carefully gave her the baby, willing the infant not to wake up and cry.

From beyond the windows she heard the sound of a helicopter and moments later Rio appeared in the doorway. His exquisitely tailored suit moulded to his athletic physique and Evie felt her stomach drop. Even after a year together, she still found it hard to breathe when he was in the same room as her.

'I'm sorry I'm late,' he drawled, dropping his briefcase and walking across to them. 'There were a few things I had to arrange. Last minute Christmas shopping. What have I missed?'

'Daddy! Have you bought my present?' Elyssa wriggled with excitement and Rio dropped a kiss on the top of her head and dropped to his haunches.

'I might have done. You're holding Lara.' He shot a questioning look at Evie who smiled reassuringly.

'Isn't she doing brilliantly? She's so good with her sister.' As she spoke, the baby's eyes opened and Evie held her breath. *Don't cry.*

'She's looking at me.' Elyssa looked at her half-sister in fascination. 'Can she see me?'

'Oh, yes.' Watching the two of them together, Evie felt a lump in her throat. 'She loves you, Elyssa.'

'Grandpa and I hung her stocking on the fireplace and I wrote to Santa to tell him she's only a baby so he doesn't leave her unsuitable toys.'

'She's so lucky having you as a big sister.' It had taken months of patience but finally the nightmares had stopped and Elyssa had started to behave like a normal little girl. Far from unsettling her, Lara's birth appeared to have given her greater security—as if the arrival of the baby had somehow cemented their little family.

Elyssa kissed Lara's downy head. 'I can't wait for her to grow big enough to be able to play with me. Can you take her back now? She's really heavy for someone who only drinks milk.'

Rio expertly scooped up his baby daughter, holding her against his shoulder as he sat down on the sofa next to Elyssa. 'Did you decorate the Christmas tree while I was away?'

'Evie wanted to wait for you.'

Knowing how Rio felt about Christmas, Evie cast him an anxious look. It was enough for her that they were together and in England. She was still overwhelmed by his decision to buy the beautiful old Manor House close to the Cedar Court Retirement Home, meaning that she could have her grandfather to stay. He'd declared himself too old to be flying around the world to visit their other homes, so Rio had shifted his business operation to enable him to spend as much time in England as possible.

And her grandfather was delighted that his wish had been fulfilled twice over. He now had two great-grandchildren to hold on his knee.

Rio leaned across Elyssa and delivered a lingering kiss to Evie's lips. 'I missed you. No more work,' he promised, 'for the whole of Christmas. Anyone who phones me is fired.'

'I missed you, too.' She kissed him back, careful not to squash the baby. 'Are you serious? You're not working?'

'I have better things to do with my time. Put your coats on. We're going outside. I have a surprise for you both.'

'Outside?' Excited, Elyssa jumped to her feet. 'Can Lara come, too?'

'Not this time. We're leaving her with Grandpa for a moment.'

Evie's grandfather was obviously in on the surprise because he timed his entrance perfectly. 'Elyssa, there's someone at the front door for you.'

Elyssa shot out of the room and Rio took Evie's hand in his and followed. 'I hope you're not going to be mad with me—'

'That depends on what you've done.' Her eyes teased him and he kissed her again, unable to leave her alone.

'I may have gone a little overboard,' he confessed, 'but, after years of not celebrating Christmas, I'm determined to make up for it big time.'

Overwhelmed with love for him, Evie lifted her hand and stroked his hair. 'I wasn't sure how you'd feel this year—that's why we haven't decorated the tree. I thought you might rather we didn't.' Hesitant, she watched him. 'I know the whole thing has bad memories for you.'

'I'm making new memories—' he captured her hand in his, his voice husky '—with you.'

'Daddy, come on!' Elyssa was waiting impatiently and Rio released Evie and walked to the front door.

'Close your eyes and don't peep until I say so.'

Elyssa squeezed them shut. 'Can I look yet?'

Rio opened the door of the house. '*Now* you can look.'

Evie watched as the little girl opened her eyes. Wonder and happiness lit her whole face. Intrigued as to what had caused such a response, Evie turned her head and gasped as she saw the pretty white pony. He stood quietly, his breath clouding the air, a big red bow in his mane. Behind him was a sleigh piled high with presents.

'Daddy!' Elyssa could hardly speak. 'Oh, Daddy!'

Rio looked smug. 'You like him?'

'He's *mine*? Truly?'

'All yours.' Rio scooped her into his arms and carried her to the pony. 'His name is Snowflake and he's the latest member of our ever-growing family. It's a good job we have a large house.'

Elyssa had her arms around the pony, almost sobbing with excitement. 'He's so beautiful. Oh—oh—Mummy, have you seen him?'

Mummy.

Rio inhaled sharply and so did Evie because she'd waited

for this moment for so long. For almost a year she'd been encouraging the withdrawn, confused little girl to call her Mummy and finally now, on Christmas Eve, she'd said it. To hear her use the word so naturally felt like a miracle.

The best Christmas gift of all.

Warmth spread through her body and Evie walked across to Rio and took Elyssa from him, hugging her tightly, tears on her face.

'I see him, sweetheart, and I think he's completely perfect.'

Her grandfather appeared in the doorway, smiling his approval as he looked at Evie with her family.

Rio looked ridiculously pleased with himself. 'It's cold out here and neither of you are properly dressed. We'll go back inside and get wrapped up and then we can go round to the stables and see Snowflake and his friends.'

Evie glanced up at him. 'Friends?'

A smile transformed his face from handsome to breathtaking. 'I bought a few spares. I have a feeling we're going to be needing them before too long.'

Evie's heart stumbled. He wanted more children. A big family.

Her dream come true.

As she smiled up at him she felt something cold brush against her face and Elyssa gave a squeal of excitement that made the pony throw up his head in alarm.

'It's snowing! Mummy, Daddy, we're going to have snow for Christmas. Can we build a snowman? Do you know how?'

Rio brushed the snow from Evie's cheek. 'Yes, I know how. We need a carrot and some pebbles and a few twigs. And we need your mother because she's brilliant at building snowmen.'

'We also need enough snow,' Evie pointed out practically.

'We need to find something to do while we're waiting for it to settle.'

'I think I can solve that problem.' Rio pulled her back into his arms and held her tightly. 'How would you feel about decorating a Christmas tree?'

MILLS & BOON

NOVEMBER 2010 HARDBACK TITLES

ROMANCE

The Dutiful Wife	Penny Jordan
His Christmas Virgin	Carole Mortimer
Public Marriage, Private Secrets	Helen Bianchin
Forbidden or For Bedding?	Julia James
The Twelve Nights of Christmas	Sarah Morgan
In Christofides' Keeping	Abby Green
The Italian's Blushing Gardener	Christina Hollis
The Socialite and the Cattle King	Lindsay Armstrong
Tabloid Affair, Secretly Pregnant!	Mira Lyn Kelly
Maharaja's Mistress	Susan Stephens
Christmas with her Boss	Marion Lennox
Firefighter's Doorstep Baby	Barbara McMahon
Daddy by Christmas	Patricia Thayer
Christmas Magic on the Mountain	Melissa McClone
A FAIRYTALE CHRISTMAS	Susan Meier & Barbara Wallace
The Soldier's Untamed Heart	Nikki Logan
Dr Zinetti's Snowkissed Bride	Sarah Morgan
The Christmas Baby Bump	Lynne Marshall

HISTORICAL

Courting Miss Vallois	Gail Whitiker
Reprobate Lord, Runaway Lady	Isabelle Goddard
The Bride Wore Scandal	Helen Dickson

MEDICAL™

Christmas in Bluebell Cove	Abigail Gordon
The Village Nurse's Happy-Ever-After	Abigail Gordon
The Most Magical Gift of All	Fiona Lowe
Christmas Miracle: A Family	Dianne Drake

1010 Gen Std LP

MILLS & BOON

NOVEMBER 2010 LARGE PRINT TITLES

ROMANCE

A Night, A Secret...A Child	Miranda Lee
His Untamed Innocent	Sara Craven
The Greek's Pregnant Lover	Lucy Monroe
The Mélendez Forgotten Marriage	Melanie Milburne
Australia's Most Eligible Bachelor	Margaret Way
The Bridesmaid's Secret	Fiona Harper
Cinderella: Hired by the Prince	Marion Lennox
The Sheikh's Destiny	Melissa James

HISTORICAL

The Earl's Runaway Bride	Sarah Mallory
The Wayward Debutante	Sarah Elliott
The Laird's Captive Wife	Joanna Fulford

MEDICAL™

The Surgeon's Miracle	Caroline Anderson
Dr Di Angelo's Baby Bombshell	Janice Lynn
Newborn Needs a Dad	Dianne Drake
His Motherless Little Twins	Dianne Drake
Wedding Bells for the Village Nurse	Abigail Gordon
Her Long-Lost Husband	Josie Metcalfe

MILLS & BOON®

DECEMBER 2010 HARDBACK TITLES

ROMANCE

Naive Bride, Defiant Wife	Lynne Graham
Nicolo: The Powerful Sicilian	Sandra Marton
Stranded, Seduced...Pregnant	Kim Lawrence
Shock: One-Night Heir	Melanie Milburne
Innocent Virgin, Wild Surrender	Anne Mather
Her Last Night of Innocence	India Grey
Captured and Crowned	Janette Kenny
Buttoned-Up Secretary, British Boss	Susanne James
Surf, Sea and a Sexy Stranger	Heidi Rice
Wild Nights with her Wicked Boss	Nicola Marsh
Mistletoe and the Lost Stiletto	Liz Fielding
Rescued by his Christmas Angel	Cara Colter
Angel of Smoky Hollow	Barbara McMahon
Christmas at Candlebark Farm	Michelle Douglas
The Cinderella Bride	Barbara Wallace
Single Father, Surprise Prince!	Raye Morgan
A Christmas Knight	Kate Hardy
The Nurse Who Saved Christmas	Janice Lynn

HISTORICAL

Lady Arabella's Scandalous Marriage	Carole Mortimer
Dangerous Lord, Seductive Miss	Mary Brendan
Bound to the Barbarian	Carol Townend
Bought: The Penniless Lady	Deborah Hale

MEDICAL™

St Piran's: The Wedding of The Year	Caroline Anderson
St Piran's: Rescuing Pregnant Cinderella	Carol Marinelli
The Midwife's Christmas Miracle	Jennifer Taylor
The Doctor's Society Sweetheart	Lucy Clark

MILLS & BOON

DECEMBER 2010 LARGE PRINT TITLES

ROMANCE

The Pregnancy Shock	Lynne Graham
Falco: The Dark Guardian	Sandra Marton
One Night...Nine-Month Scandal	Sarah Morgan
The Last Kolovsky Playboy	Carol Marinelli
Doorstep Twins	Rebecca Winters
The Cowboy's Adopted Daughter	Patricia Thayer
SOS: Convenient Husband Required	Liz Fielding
Winning a Groom in 10 Dates	Cara Colter

HISTORICAL

Rake Beyond Redemption	Anne O'Brien
A Thoroughly Compromised Lady	Bronwyn Scott
In the Master's Bed	Blythe Gifford
Bought: The Penniless Lady	Deborah Hale

MEDICAL™

The Midwife and the Millionaire	Fiona McArthur
From Single Mum to Lady	Judy Campbell
Knight on the Children's Ward	Carol Marinelli
Children's Doctor, Shy Nurse	Molly Evans
Hawaiian Sunset, Dream Proposal	Joanna Neil
Rescued: Mother and Baby	Anne Fraser